THEY CALLED HIM LIGHTNING

A blow to the head had caused him memory loss and temporary blindness. Was he Mike Clancey, the name inscribed on the pocket watch he carried? And the beautiful woman's picture on the inside of the watch — was she his wife? He needed answers. Known as Lightning for his gun skills, riding Thunder, a black gelding, with fair play and talent he would bring a tyrant to justice — but it was a dangerous trail he must follow.

MARK FALCON

THEY CALLED HIM LIGHTNING

Complete and Unabridged

LINFORD
Leicester

First published in Great Britain in 2007 by
Robert Hale Limited
London

First Linford Edition
published 2008
by arrangement with
Robert Hale Limited
London

The moral right of the author has been asserted

British Library CIP Data

Falcon, Mark
    They called him Lightning.—Large print ed.—
Linford western library
    1. Western stories
    2. Large type books
    I. Title
    823.9′2 [F]

ISBN 978–1–84782–127–0

Published by
F. A. Thorpe (Publishing)
Anstey, Leicestershire

Set by Words & Graphics Ltd.
Anstey, Leicestershire
Printed and bound in Great Britain by
T. J. International Ltd., Padstow, Cornwall

This book is printed on acid-free paper

For Janet Jackson Karunaratne
and in memory of
John Pickering 1801–1875
and
Trefina Pickering 1837–1845

1

The jet-black horse stopped on the brow of the hill without any prompting from its master. The rider took out the silver watch from the pocket of his shirt and looked at it once more. The metal was beginning to look worn from handling. The fair-haired man opened it up and gazed down again at the picture of a dark-haired young woman on the inside of the lid. He had become tired of wondering who she could be. Maybe he would never know. Maybe also he would never know his own name. On the back of the watch was inscribed:

TO MIKE CLANCEY
WITH GRATEFUL THANKS
FROM
LODESTONE

The rider had begun to think of

himself as Mike Clancey. Unless he had stolen the watch, he guessed it must be his, so Mike Clancey must be his name. But he could not be sure of that. He had been given another name over the past six months — *Lightning*.

As he had gone on his way throughout Texas, he had searched for answers to his questions. Sometimes the people he had asked had forced him to defend himself — and they found out the hard way that this man was not one to be trifled with.

Mike — or Lightning — looked down on the dusty road below. Which way this time? he wondered. In the distance, to his right, he noticed dust rising into the air, and a few seconds later, another haze of dust. He waited, and watched.

Soon a horse-drawn wagon came into view and a short while later he was able to make out that the driver was a woman, whose long dark hair streamed back behind her. Then he realized why she was in such a big hurry. Four riders were coming up closer to her, soon to overtake her just below him.

Two of the men caught hold of the horse's reins and forced it to stop. Another dismounted and climbed up next to the woman. She went for her rifle by her side, but the man was too quick and snatched it from her before she could use it. The fourth rider had begun to throw out the provisions in the wagon down on to the ground, first slitting open the sacks and laughing as the flour and grain mingled with the dust.

Mike drew his .45 and nudged his mount down the hill. He had already made sure that it was not too steep a gradient for the horse.

By now the man on the wagon had pulled the woman to the ground and was intent on molesting her. Mike heard the material of her shirt rip.

He let off a bullet which went through the man's calf. The scream he made told Mike he had done some damage.

The other three men began to draw their guns but Mike's gun barked three times in rapid succession, each bullet hitting the men in their gun hands.

All four men wore bandannas over their faces. Mike dismounted and kicked their guns away from them. He pulled down the cloth to reveal the faces of the three nearest him.

Keeping his gun levelled at the four, he took a quick look at the woman, who by now had got to her feet. He could see that she was badly shaken.

'What are your names?' Mike asked the men. He received no answer. He noticed that the one with the bullet in his leg was about to draw his gun.

'Throw it over here!' Mike ordered. 'And don't try to use it or my next bullet will go in your heart.'

The man hesitated but wisely decided not to try and shoot it out with this stranger who was in command.

Mike walked over to him, picked up his gun and threw it as far as he could. He then pulled down the man's bandanna to reveal his face.

The woman came up to Mike, away from the four bandits.

'Have you ever seen these men before, miss?' Mike asked.

'They're Frank Ringwald's men. Ringwald wants our property but Pa won't sell it to him. Most of our neighbours have packed up and left. They were all afraid for their lives.'

'What about the law around here? Couldn't the sheriff do something about it?'

The pretty young woman shook her head. 'He's in Ringwald's pocket. We all think he's been threatened and he's afraid for his family's safety.'

'Mm.' Mike pondered. 'Are the townsfolk made up of men, or mice?' he exclaimed.

'I guess they need a leader,' the woman said.

Mike nodded. 'I understand. You four, get on your horses and give a message to this Ringwald. Tell him if he sends any more scum like you to attack lone women or their families while I'm around, they won't return — except in pine boxes. Savvy?'

The four did not reply.

'Savvy?' Mike asked again, more loudly.

'I can't ride with this leg,' said the man who had been about to molest the woman.

'I can arrange for you to ride without it! Now git! And don't show your ugly faces around here again!'

Two of the men were about to pick up their guns but Mike's gun barked and a bullet hit the ground near their weapons. They thought better of it and left them where they were. The third man assisted the fourth into the saddle, then mounted his own horse. All four took a last look at Mike.

'Who shall we say you are?' one of them asked him.

Mike hesitated slightly before answering.

'They call me Lightning,' was his reply.

A chill ran through them all.

Mike and the girl watched while they rode off in the direction from whence they had come.

'Thank you,' said the woman with a tremble in her voice.

'Are you OK?' he asked her.

'I feel a bit shaky, but I'll get over it.'

Mike nodded.

'I'll put your provisions back in the wagon. Most of it's been spoilt though. Couldn't someone have gone into town with you?'

'Ringwald ran off our men. Only Jake stayed and he and Pa were mending fences after they'd been broken down. I didn't think anyone would bother me, so I risked going to town alone.'

Mike assisted the young woman on to the wagon after he had put the provisions back.

'I'll come with you back home. I doubt if you'll be bothered by anyone else, though.'

He mounted his horse and rode

beside her. He noticed that she looked at him a few times and guessed she was wondering about him.

'Lightning isn't your real name, is it?' she asked after a few minutes of silence between them.

'No. But I don't know my real name — for sure.'

He looked at her and noticed her lips part in surprise.

'I don't understand,' she said.

'Somehow I lost my memory. I also lost my sight for a while. Thunder here — ' he patted his horse's neck — 'brought me to a town and some of the townsfolk took care of me. I recovered my sight, but not my memory.' He gave a short laugh. 'I'm riding around looking for it.'

Mike took out the familiar watch from his vest-pocket and handed it to her.

'Have you ever seen this woman before?' he asked her.

'She's pretty,' she commented. 'No. Sorry.'

She turned the watch over and read the inscription.

'Mike Clancey,' she read out. 'This could be your name.'

'Sure. It *could* be. It might not be my watch though. Anyhow, *where* or *who* is Lodestone?'

She shook her head and frowned.

'I've never heard of Lodestone before. It could be a mining-town,' she suggested.

'I've come up with lots of *coulds* or *maybes*. I'll just have to call in on every town in Texas and ask the same questions.'

After about five miles from the place where Mike had come across the girl, a ranch house came into view.

'That's where I live,' she said.

Mike nodded.

'You haven't told me your name yet.'

'Trefina. Trefina Pickering. My pa's name's John.'

John Pickering heard the sound of the wagon and went to the door to greet his daughter. He noticed that her shirt had been torn and the top two buttons had come off. He had never seen the man riding beside her before and immediately came to the conclusion he must be one of Ringwald's men. John ducked back into the house and came out carrying a rifle which he aimed at the stranger.

'Pa! No!' Trefina screamed. 'Don't shoot!'

2

John Pickering hesitated before pulling the trigger. The man riding beside his daughter wore a gun, but he had made no attempt to draw the weapon.

'Pa, this man saved me from Ringwald's men. He escorted me back here,' Trefina told him quickly.

Pickering lowered his rifle and waited for his daughter to get down from the wagon and run up to him. The stranger did not attempt to dismount. He was a well-built man, Pickering noted. He looked tall and seemed confident.

'It seems as if I owe you an apology, mister. Come inside, I've got coffee on the stove.'

Mike nodded his thanks and dismounted, tossing Thunder's reins over the hitching-post outside the door. He followed Trefina and her father into the house. The room was large and Mike noticed that stairs led up to another floor. It was obvious that the place had been built a couple of decades or more ago and was well-furnished.

'Sit yourself down, mister. What do they call you?'

'Some people call me Lightning. Others, Mike Clancey. But I can't say for sure if that's my name.'

Pickering frowned.

'He's lost his memory, Pa,' Trefina told him. 'He's riding around Texas hoping someone knows him.'

'Is that a fact! Well I'll be darned!'

Trefina went over to the stove and poured out three mugs of coffee. She gave Mike a big smile as she handed one to him.

'What happened?' John Pickering asked them both. Trefina answered.

'I was coming back from town but I felt someone was following me. After a couple of miles I noticed four men approaching. They all wore masks over their faces, so I cracked the whip and tried to outride them. But it was no use. They overtook me and . . . and they pulled the horse to a stop and threw down the provisions. One of them . . . tried to . . . ' Trefina hung her head and was unable to finish the sentence.

'And is that when you turned up?' John asked Mike.

'Yeah. Just in time, I reckon. They won't try anything like that for a while.'

'I'm sure grateful to you, mister. Shall I call you Mike?'

'You might as well.' Mike nodded with a smile.

'Maybe we won't be bothered with Ringwald and his men from now on, Pa?' Trefina said hopefully.

John's lips drew into a thin line.

'I doubt it, Trefina. Mike here may have deterred these men, but there'll be others to do his dirty work. He won't give up until I sell him the ranch to add to all the rest of the land he's gotten his hands on.'

Mike drank some of the welcome coffee. His brow was furrowed as he mulled over Pickering's words.

'How long has this been going on, Mr Pickering?' Mike asked him.

'Call me John, son,' Pickering told him. 'About ten years now. It started when his pa died and he took over running the place. He wanted to expand and own all the ranches around him. He succeeded — except for this one.' John sighed and took a sip of coffee.

'I might as well give in,' he continued. 'I've got no one to help me run the place — Frank Ringwald saw to that by threatening my men or paying them more to join him.'

'He sounds like a bully, and all bullies are cowards deep down. He must have a weak spot. Find that, and you can work on it.'

John shot him a surprised look. He had never heard anyone talk like this before. Was there hope? he wondered. But deep down he realized he could do nothing without this stranger's help. Would he be prepared to stick around and give that help, or would he just ride off again leaving him and Trefina to face things alone? He knew he would have to find out.

'You're welcome to stay for as long as you want, Mike,' John offered hopefully.

'Thanks. I'd like to stick around for a while. Mebbe I could help out around the place for my keep?'

Mike noticed Trefina's eager smile at this before her father shook Mike's hand gratefully.

'I'd be much obliged if you would. I'd pay you. It'd be the least I could do.'

'I'll help you bring in the supplies, Trefina. What's left of them,' Mike added. 'I might pay this Ringwald fella a visit and hand him a bill for all the goods that are ruined. Which direction is his place from here?'

John pointed north-east.

'He's not at home much. You're more than likely to find him in town.' He gave a grunt of anger. 'He owns that, too — and almost everyone in it!'

Mike took out his watch again and looked at the time. Half past six.

'I'll make an early start in the morning, John. I'd like to get there by noon.'

'No, Mike.' Pickering shook his head. 'I can't let you do that. One of Ringwald's men will shoot you in the back and say it was in self-defence.'

Clancey gave a short laugh. 'No one would believe that!'

'Ringwald would make you believe black was white and white was black,' Trefina chipped in.

'Don't you worry, Trefina.' Mike smiled at her. 'I'll watch my back.'

Trefina left the two to talk while she went upstairs to change from her torn shirt and returned a few minutes later in a dress of forget-me-not blue. John Pickering noticed the appreciative look on Mike Clancey's face as she re-entered the room.

'I'll start supper,' she said. 'We need more supplies to make up for the spoilt stuff. Perhaps you'll accompany me into town when you go tomorrow, Mike?'

Mike shook his head.

'I'd rather you stayed here, Trefina,' he told her firmly. 'I'll bring back what you need. I'll take the wagon and leave Thunder here.'

John stood up and thumped the mantelshelf with his fist.

'I feel only half a man letting you do my fighting for me!' he raged. 'I should have stood up to Ringwald years ago. I don't like admitting it, Mike, but I'm nothing but a coward.'

Clancey shook his head sadly.

'No, you're not, John. If you got yourself shot, who would take care of Trefina? Mebbe if you hadn't anyone to look out for you would have fought back, but there's only one of you against his men. I guess he's got more than the four that attacked Trefina today?'

John nodded. 'Many more. He wouldn't dare go around without a gang of men accompanying him. I guess he's more of a coward than I am.'

Clancey nodded enthusiastically.

'You said it, John.'

After supper Clancey stood up and stretched his long arms out.

'I think I'll hit the hay. The bunkhouse will do.'

Trefina gave a quick look at her father before speaking.

'We've got a spare room upstairs. You are our guest.'

'Thanks, but the bunkhouse will do fine. Make out a bill for the spoilt goods and I'll replace them tomorrow in town. Goodnight, folks. And thanks for supper. It was very good.'

Trefina and John watched as Mike Clancey walked across to the bunkhouse, saw him open the door and go inside.

John felt his daughter's hands around his arm.

'Pa, I'm scared. Scared for him in town tomorrow. If only we'd got some men of our own to go with him.'

John took his daughter in his arms

and held her close to his chest.

'I feel the same, girl. Mebbe Jake will come with me and give him back-up?'

'Pa, if you go into town tomorrow, so will I. I can use a gun — a rifle at least.'

'No! I forbid it!' John emphasized. 'We'd be looking out for you instead of being any help to Clancey.'

★　★　★

Mike entered the bunkhouse and noticed a Negro lying on the top of the far bunk, smoking a brier pipe.

''Evenin',' the man said amiably.

Mike guessed this must be Jake, the last man to stay with John Pickering.

''Evenin',' Mike replied with a smile. 'I guess I can have any one of the bunks?' Mike swept the room with his hand at the two rows of bunks which had not been used for some time.

'Sure,' Jake answered. 'Any one at all. I guess you've had supper?'

Mike nodded. 'Good it was, too. Do you ever join them?'

19

'Sometimes,' said Jake. 'Somtimes I cook it for them if they want me to.'

Mike nodded.

'I'll see to my horse, then I'll get my head down. I need to be fresh for the morning. There's much to do in town. There could be trouble.'

Jake's brow furrowed as the tall stranger left the bunkhouse to put his mount in the stable for the night. A shiver ran down his back at the man's words.

3

Clancey awoke early the next morning to the smell of fresh coffee and sizzling bacon. Jake had been busy.

'Breakfast's ready, mister. I didn't catch your name last night.'

Clancey grinned. 'That's because I didn't give it. My friends call me Mike Clancey.'

Jake's thick lips turned up slightly.

'And what do your enemies call you?'

'I've been called Lightning more than once.' Mike noticed Jake's eyes flash to the gunbelt he was strapping on with the .45 snugly in its holster. The Negro nodded.

After breakfast Mike called in at the house for the bill for the spoilt goods which he intended handing to Ringwald.

'I can't let you go into town alone, Mike,' said John. 'I'll come with you.'

Mike shook his head.

'I work best alone, John. Expect me back by nightfall. But if I'm not back,' he added, 'you'll know something's happened to me.'

John went with him to the barn. He brought out the horse and hitched it up to the wagon.

Mike's horse nickered at the sight of its master.

'Sorry, Thunder, you can rest up for the day.'

Trefina came to the door as Mike climbed aboard the wagon. She looked worried, Mike thought. She was a very pretty young woman and Mike wondered why no young man had not snapped her up before now.

Mike moved off and gave them a wave. Jake had come up to see him off also.

'Do you reckon he'll be OK, Mr John?'

Pickering looked fondly at the old man.

'I sure as hell hope so, Jake.'

It felt strange to Mike to be travelling aboard a wagon and not in the saddle. He looked up at the sun and then at his watch. It was seven o'clock. He hoped to reach town by noon.

★　★　★

The sun was at its zenith when Mike reached town. He had judged the journey-time well. He noticed the signboard pointing the way to the buildings ahead. It read Ringwald. A grim smile crossed Mike's sunbronzed face. Now why am not surprised? he asked himself. The Pickerings had told him Ringwald owned the town, so it was logical that he would name it after himself.

Ringwald contained all the stores and services that were necessary for it to survive. The saloon was placed midway down the right hand side of the street. Mike drew up outside and jumped down from the wagon.

He pushed open the batwing doors.

The saloon was full. He stood and surveyed the room, hoping to pick out Ringwald in the crowd.

As he strode up to the bar, Mike could feel everyone's eyes upon him. He had become used to this. Obviously his description had been given by the four cowards he had dealt with the day before.

'Beer,' Mike said to the barman.

The glass was put before him and Mike handed over a dollar.

'Is Ringwald in here?' Mike asked.

'*Mr* Ringwald,' the barman emphasized.

Mike ignored this.

'Wal, is he?'

'At the far table.' The man pointed. 'Dark-haired with the string bow tie.'

Mike gave the barman a curt nod of acknowledgement and carried his beer across to the table indicated.

'Mr Ringwald?' Mike asked the described man.

Mike's presence had not been missed by him.

'You must be the one they call Lightning,' Ringwald stated, rather than asked.

Mike nodded. 'I have been called that on more than one occasion. I've got a bill here for you,' he said, producing the piece of paper given to him by John Pickering.

'What for?' Ringwald asked with no apparent interest.

'For all the damaged goods your four flunkies caused yesterday when they attacked Miss Pickering and her wagon.'

'That has nothing to do with me,' said Ringwald as he placed a card from the hand he was playing down on the deck.

'They were *your* men, carrying out *your* orders, Ringwald. Otherwise, how would you know what people call me? If I hadn't come along when I did, Miss Pickering would have been . . . seriously molested by those men. It was a cowardly act and I expect you, as their employer, to pay for it. For the goods, if nothing else.'

'As I've just said — what happened had nothing to do with me. Anyhow, you got your revenge. All four are no use to me after you shot them.'

Mike noticed that the man had not looked him in the eyes once while he spoke. He knew a man could never be trusted unless he did.

'The amount's for twenty dollars.' Mike slapped the paper with the back of his right hand.

'I don't care a damn how much it's for. Get out of my sight before I have you arrested!'

Mike sensed uneasy movement behind and around him. He had been called out in not so many words. Ringwald appeared confident that he would not be shot down amongst so many people as witnesses.

The movement was barely seen, but suddenly a gun appeared in Mike's hand. He glanced down at the pile of money on the table.

Mike took off his hat and quickly gathered the money into it.

'There looks to be about that amount here, Mr Ringwald. I'll trouble you no further now the debt has been paid. Good day to you. I'll tell Miss Pickering that you're sorry what happened to her yesterday — shall I?'

Mike backed away, glancing from left to right as he did so. He had just reached the door, his back still to it, when everything went black.

*   *   *

Mike opened his eyes and his head hurt like hell. He eased himself up with his elbows and found that he was lying on a bunk. Bars were across one wall of the small room. He realized that he was in a jail cell.

He needed a drink as his mouth felt as dry as dust. What had happened to him? How long had he been in there? He could hear talking coming from an adjacent room. He strained his ears to try and hear what they were saying, but the words were indistinct. Maybe he couldn't hear because of the drumming in his head.

How long would it be before someone came to take a look at him? he wondered. Should he shout, or wait?

After a while someone entered the room outside his cell. The man wore a sheriff's badge.

'Oh, so you're still with us?' the portly man said.

'What am I doing here?' Mike asked him weakly, the words barely audible from his parched throat.

'I arrested you for robbing Mr Ringwald's poker game,' came the explanation.

Mike thought hard for a few moments.

'Robbed?' he asked.

'Don't you remember?'

Mike shook his head, and wished he hadn't.

'What's your name?' the sheriff asked him.

'I can't remember,' he answered.

'Don't give me that!' scoffed the lawman.

'I tell you I don't know. Give me a drink.' Mike felt the back of his head. It had obviously bled but the blood was now dry.

'You're in luck,' said the sheriff. 'My deputy has just made a fresh pot of coffee.'

He left the room and returned a moment or two later with a mug which he handed to Mike through the bars.

'Maybe that'll refresh your memory,' the sheriff suggested.

Mike took a sip, then another.

'I doubt it.'

'OK.' The lawman sighed. 'You can stay right there until your memory returns.'

Mike pursed his lips into a thin line.

'That might take a lot longer than you think, Sheriff.'

★   ★   ★

It was now dark and Mike Clancey had not returned to the Pickering ranch. Trefina looked up at her father and he

29

could see how worried she was feeling. He was beginning to feel the same.

'Pa, we've got to find out what's happened to him,' Trefina pleaded.

John nodded. 'If he's not here by midday tomorrow, we'll go look for him. Maybe he stayed in town over-night?' he suggested hopefully.

Trefina nodded. 'Maybe. But what if he stayed against his will?'

4

Frank Ringwald strode through the door to the cell room. Mike looked up and vaguely remembered the face. His head still ached and his vision was blurred.

'The sheriff tells me you won't give your name,' he stated as he looked down at Clancey who was sitting on the bunk with his head in his hands.

'I would if I knew it,' was Mike's reply.

'Do you mean that crack on the head you got has made you forget?' Ringwald asked sceptically.

'No,' said Mike, 'but it didn't help none. I haven't been sure of my name for some time.'

Ringwald frowned. 'How's that?'

Mike shrugged his broad shoulders.

'Another crack on the head made me forget everything. You don't know a place called Lodestone, do you by any chance?'

Ringwald shook his head and frowned again.

'I've come to put a proposition to you.'

'And what's that?' Mike asked warily.

'Come and work for me. I could use someone with your particular skills — especially after you put four of my best men out of action. I pay well,' Ringwald added.

Mike looked him squarely in the face.

'What would I have to do to receive such good wages?'

'Take care of all my many businesses, and also be my right-hand man.'

A smile crossed Clancey's lips.

'In other words, someone to watch your back.'

'Yeah. That just about describes it,' said Ringwald.

Mike thought he detected a smile cross the man's lips; a rare sight, he imagined.

'I think mebbe you're asking the

wrong man, Ringwald.'

The smile quickly disappeared from Ringwald's lips.

'You will refer to me as *Mr* Ringwald!' he told him angrily. 'No one calls me just Ringwald.'

'Is that so?' Mike replied with another smile of contempt.

'Well?' Ringwald asked. 'What's your decision?'

'My decision is . . . ' Mike hesitated. 'My decision is . . . Do you know, I've damn well forgotten what my decision is. I'll think it over.' And with that, Mike turned over on the bunk with his back to Ringwald.

Ringwald ground his teeth together in anger. No one had ever spoken to him like this before and he did not like it.

'Don't take too long, man with no name. If I don't receive a favourable reply by morning, you can stay here and rot. And I *mean* that!' With that, Ringwald stomped out of the cell room.

Before Clancey closed his eyes in an

attempt to get rid of his headache, he began to feel slightly worried. They had relieved him of his .45 and he was locked in this cell. Now he was unable to help John and Trefina Pickering. Perhaps his intervention had made it worse for them both.

★   ★   ★

John and Trefina Pickering and Jake tried to continue their chores on the ranch as usual, but each knew that the others were worrying about the non-appearance of Mike Clancey.

At last it was noon. They all looked at each other in turn.

'He's not back, Pa,' said Trefina unnecessarily.

John made a decision.

'Right, Jake, we'll go and find out what's happened to him.'

'I'm not staying here on my own, Pa. I'm coming with you.'

John looked at his daughter and she could see the quandary he was in.

'OK, Trefina. Go and dress for riding!'

She quickly ran into the house to change into a divided skirt and shirt.

When Trefina came outside a few minutes later she saw that three horses were saddled. John and Jake mounted up and John handed Trefina the reins to her brown mare.

'It'll be dusk before we get to town,' said John.

'Under cover of darkness, eh, Pa?' Trefina smiled slightly as she looked across at her father.

'We'll need a way to find out where Lightning is, Mr John,' said Jake. 'And at the same time we musn't draw attention to ourselves.'

Pickering nodded. 'By the time we reach town, I hope one of us will have come up with a plan.'

★　★　★

The three had now reached the outskirts of town. They knew the stores would be closed but the saloon was occupied both day and night and the sound of a piano being thumped into a tune came to their ears.

'Look, Pa.' Trefina pointed ahead. 'That's our horse and wagon outside the saloon. It looks as though he's spent all this time in there. And I thought we could trust him!'

John sensed the disappointment in his daughter's voice.

'We can't be sure of that,' he answered. 'It's obvious that he went in there . . . ' His voice trailed off as he thought about it. 'We can't be sure though, that he's still in there. He might have met with . . . an accident?'

Trefina felt her heartbeats quicken. Her father's words were painting a sinister picture in her mind.

'Pa,' Trefina began, 'we could go round the back of the buildings and then maybe we wouldn't be noticed.'

John Pickering nodded and smiled.

'That seems like a good idea, Trefina. We'll try that.'

The three rode to their right and dismounted at the back of the hardware store. There was no one around. Only the road through town was busy.

'Trefina, stay here with the horses. Jake, come with me. We'll get into the saloon from the back way and take a look inside. If Mike's not there, we'll have to assume that he's somewhere else.'

As the two men walked off, Jake looked at his boss.

'The funeral parlour or the jail comes to mind.'

They found the back entrance to the saloon. There were no windows here and the place was in total darkness.

John walked up to the door and tried it. He half-expected it to be locked, but on trying the knob, he found that it opened. He nodded to Jake, who stepped up close to him.

The two men entered the building silently, feeling their way around the room until they came to another door. The sound of the piano now became louder to them and they guessed this door led into the saloon itself.

John turned the knob slowly and a vertical slit of light showed.

As he opened the door wider, he found himself in a hallway behind the stairs leading to the rooms above. The stairs gave him good cover as he surveyed the room. Jake stepped through the doorway and stood by his side. They were sure no one had noticed them as their eyes took in every inch of the noisy, smoke-filled room ahead of them. But they were wrong.

A tall, good-looking cowboy was sitting at one of the tables, a beer in his right hand. He happened to look up at that moment and noticed two men standing by the stairs. He recognized them instantly. The old Negro was Jake and the other was his former boss, John Pickering.

Ben Haines gave no indication that he had seen the two and lowered his eyes. He now worked for Frank Ringwald, but he wished he didn't. The pay was certainly better than he had received from John Pickering, but he still felt ashamed of walking out on his former boss. Ringwald was a bully and a coward. Ben ground his teeth in anger as he thought over how Ringwald had sent four of his men to harass Trefina Pickering on her way back home from town. He had learned how they had tried to do more than that, and would have succeeded if a stranger had not intervened. The stranger was at that moment in the jail and he guessed he was the one whom John Pickering and Jake had come looking for. He thought about Trefina and became even more angry at Ringwald for sending his men out to molest her, and angry at himself for sitting back and letting it happen.

Ben had never spoken to Trefina, except to say 'Good-morning', but he held the young woman in high regard. To him she was like a goddess, an unattainable goddess.

He saw that Pickering and Jake had gone back the way they had come. Ben

Haines drank the last of his beer and left the saloon by the door leading to the main street. He made his way to the back of the buildings and in the gloom, noticed a girl with long, dark hair standing beside three horses. It must be Trefina, he guessed.

Trefina waited patiently for the return of her father and Jake. They seemed to be taking a long time. What if Ringwald noticed them? She was sure that if he did he would have them arrested on some trumped-up charge.

She was growing uneasy, wondering whether she should follow them and find out what had happened.

It was then that she felt an arm come around her from behind and a large hand closed over her mouth, suppressing any scream.

'Keep quiet!' came the order.

5

John and Jake shut the door to the rear of the saloon silently behind them. They looked towards Trefina and both jumped with alarm at seeing her held by a man who had a hand over her mouth. In the dim light they could not identify him.

John's hand went for his gun and Jake followed suit. Both realized that it was useless to shoot or Trefina would get hit. Also, the shot would alert the rest of Ringwald's men.

'I don't mean her any harm, Mr Pickering,' the man explained. 'It's me — Ben Haines.'

'Haines!' Pickering snarled. 'Still doing Ringwald's dirty work for him?'

John and Jake moved forward, their guns still in their hands. They noticed that Haines had not drawn his own weapon.

'I just didn't want Miss Trefina to call out. I'm through with Ringwald. I'm sorry I left you like I did.' He released Trefina and stood back so that the two men could see that he did not attempt to go for his gun.

'You've come looking for that Lightnin' feller, I reckon?' said Haines.

'Sure.' Pickering nodded. 'Any idea where we can find him?'

'He's in the jail. He wanted Ringwald to pay for the damage to the supplies in Miss Trefina's wagon. When Mr Ringwald refused to pay, Lightning collected the money up from the poker-table into his hat. He'd nearly reached the door, backing out while covering the room with his gun. At that moment the deputy walked in and cracked him on the back of his head with the butt of his gun. He dropped like a stone and he was carried into the jail.'

'I see,' said Pickering, rubbing his chin thoughtfully. 'I want him out. Will you help us do it, Haines?'

'I'll surely try, Mr Pickering.'

Haines looked down at Trefina's pretty face, upturned to him in the dim light. How he wished he could crush her to him and kiss her hard on that sweet mouth of hers.

The three men and Trefina walked along the back of the buildings until they came to the jailhouse. They noticed a small, barred opening high up in the wall.

'Is that the only cell?' Pickering asked Haines.

'Yes, it's one big cell. It only has two bunks but could hold about six prisoners. Lightning's the only one at the moment.'

'Good,' said Pickering. 'I have an idea.'

All three looked at him expectantly.

'If we tie a rope — or two or three ropes — around those bars and pull . . . '

Trefina's face lit up.

'Maybe if we were mounted and tied the ropes round the saddle horns, the horses would be able to pull harder?' she suggested.

Pickering gave a short laugh.

'Come on, let's get the horses.'

'Mr John,' Jake began hesitantly, 'don't you reckon someone ought to distract the deputy on duty in there? Pulling the bars outa the walls will surely make a noise.'

The three looked at Haines at this suggestion.

'Sure, I'll cause some distraction,' Haines offered.

'But can we trust you?' Trefina asked. 'You ran out on us once. What's to say you won't betray us again?'

'Miss Trefina, I feel mighty guilty at what I've done. Please believe me, I won't let you down again — I promise on my dead mother's grave.'

'OK.' Pickering nodded. 'We'll start tying the ropes around the bars, by which time you ought to have got round to the jail. Tell the deputy that Ringwald sent you to check on Lightning. Don't let him go into the cell, though.'

Ben Haines touched his hat in acknowledgement and walked off to the front of the jail.

John, Trefina and Jake brought their horses up to the cell. John needed to be mounted to reach the bars. He wrapped the coiled rope around one of them. Jake did likewise, but Trefina, on her smaller mare, could not quite reach up to them. John took the rope from her and tied it firmly then handed it back to her. By the time Trefina had wrapped it round the pommel a few times and tied it, John reckoned that Ben Haines would have arrived at the jail. He was right.

Haines walked into the jail and sat down in a chair facing the deputy.

''Evenin', Charlie. Everything quiet?' he asked.

Charlie Cross looked up at the cowboy now sitting opposite him, and nodded.

'Sure.' He jerked his head towards the cell. 'I don't reckon I'll get any trouble from him tonight.' He gave a short laugh. 'I musta knocked all the lightning outa him. He can't even remember his name.'

'If you want to call in at the saloon for a while, I'll sit here and guard this place,' Ben offered.

A smile crossed the deputy's lips.

'Mighty good of you, Ben. I don't mind if I do.'

Charlie wasted no time hanging around. He picked up his hat and left the sheriff's office. Ben walked over to the door and watched the skinny man hurry over to the saloon.

Ben quickly snatched up the key to the cell and went through the door leading to the room. The man called Lightning was lying on a bunk with his back to him. Ben unlocked the cell door and went inside.

Lightning still lay still.

'Hey, hurry up and get outa here before the deputy gets back!' he said in a low voice.

There was no movement from the prisoner so Ben gave him a shake.

Lightning mumbled and half-turned his head slowly towards Ben.

'Come on, hurry it up!' Ben pleaded.

Lightning pulled himself up on to his elbows and hoisted himself up from the bunk.

'Yeah, and as soon as I walk out this door, I'll be plugged in the back. 'Killed whilst trying to escape'.'

Ben gave a sigh of impatience and lit a lantern on a table outside the open cell door.

'Look up there!' He pointed at the small hole in the wall which let in a little light from outside. 'See them ropes attached to the bars?'

Lightning looked up to where Ben was pointing and frowned.

'It's Mr Pickering, Trefina and Jake. They think you'll be able to get out of that hole if they pull the bars out, but looking at you, you'll be too big to get through. Come on, I won't shoot you.'

Lightning looked him in the eyes to determine whether he was lying or not. The cowboy had not drawn his gun

— but was this just to make him walk out into an ambush?

As they reached the sheriff's office Ben looked around for Lightning's gunbelt. It was lying on top of a cabinet. He quickly grabbed hold of it and handed it to the former prisoner.

'You'll find Mr Pickering round the back with Trefina and Jake.'

At that moment they heard the sound of the bars to the cell being pulled out.

Ben opened the door to the street and looked up and down. There was no sign of any of Ringwald's men.

By now, Lightning had buckled on his gunbelt.

'I used to work for Mr Pickering and I wish I'd never left him. You can trust me, Lightning. Now go! And make it quick! I'll stay here and lock the cell again. They'll think you got outa the hole.'

Lightning touched Ben's arm in thanks, and quickly made his way round the back of the buildings.

He could see three figures ahead of

him, all mounted. He hurried to them.

'Thanks, but I chose the easier way out.' He grinned at them, revealing white teeth in the darkness.

'How did you escape?' Pickering asked in amazement.

'A young cowboy you sent to help me. He's waiting in the sheriff's office for the deputy to return from the saloon.'

A sudden thought occurred to him.

'Darn it!' Mike said. 'He gave me back my gun. They'll know he helped me to escape when they see it gone.'

'When Ringwald finds out, I don't reckon much for his chances,' said Trefina.

They all looked at her and knew she was right.

'I'll need a horse,' Mike reminded them. 'You didn't bring Thunder with you by any chance?'

They shook their heads.

'Dare we risk the horse and wagon still waiting outside the saloon?' Trefina asked.

'Go on ahead, you three,' said Mike 'I've got my gun back and I'll bring that young cowboy along with me. He won't be safe when they find out I'm missing.'

John Pickering nodded, but he did not intend leaving without Mike. They would wait for him just outside town.

6

Mike checked his gun and refilled the chamber with four bullets, making six with the two already in there.

He walked along the sidewalk to the sheriff's office and looked in at the window. Ben Haines was still there, alone. The young cowboy looked up as Mike entered, surprise showing on his face.

'What the hell are you doing back here, Lightning? I thought you'd be well away by now.'

'I would've been,' Mike replied, 'but we forgot one thing before I left. I took my gun so they'd be sure to know you helped me to escape. Come on, let's go — before the deputy gets back.'

Ben hesitated for a few seconds.

'Come on!' Mike urged impatiently. 'We've got no time to lose.'

Ben picked up his hat, put it on and

followed Mike out of the door.

'Where's your horse?' Mike asked him.

'Outside the saloon.'

Mike hurried towards the place and jumped up on the wagon. He felt sorry for the horse who had been standing there patiently since the day before.

Ben mounted up and at the same time Charlie Cross came through the batwing doors.

'Hey, Ben, where you goin'?' the deputy called.

Ben made no reply and turned his mount around. Mike had turned the wagon to face the Pickering ranch. He slapped the reins over the horse's back and yelled it onwards.

It took the deputy a few seconds to realize what was happening, then he recognized his erstwhile prisoner. When it eventually sank into his slightly intoxicated brain, he went back inside the saloon and called for help to catch the two.

By the time several men had

mounted up, Ben and Mike were well out of town. At the bend in the road they noticed John Pickering, Trefina and Jake waiting for them.

'Come on! They're close on our tails,' Mike yelled as he passed by them on the wagon.

'How many of them are after us?' Trefina asked as they came up alongside.

'Sorry, didn't stop to count.' Mike flashed her a smile to try and alleviate her fears.

They raced through the night, the stars up above giving them some light to see by.

'Lightning,' Ben began hesitantly, 'I don't want to worry you none, but we won't be safe at the ranch. If Ringwald is with them, he'll make them burn the place down — with us all inside.'

'Mebbe we'd better take cover and shoot it out before we get home?' John suggested.

'Yeah, I was thinking along those lines myself,' said Mike.

'Trefina, swap places with me. Carry on home in the wagon and we'll lie in wait for them behind those boulders.' Mike pointed to the side of them.

Trefina jumped down and hurried to the wagon. She climbed up. Mike led her mare behind the boulders and was joined by the three men.

'Trefina, make for the cave in the hills,' her father told her. 'You'll be safer there.'

'Yes, Pa,' she replied, and cracked the reins down on the horse's back.

Only a few minutes later they heard the approaching posse.

'Take careful aim,' Mike told them. 'Make every bullet count.'

They were unable to recognize the men. Mike wondered whether Ringwald was among them, or had he sent his men to do his bidding?

There were more men than Mike had expected. He shot down the first one and the others scattered to evade the bullets. Pickering shot down another of them but was sure he was not dead, merely wounded.

'Keep riding!' one of the posse shouted out.

Jake fired a shot at the retreating figures, but was sure he had not hit anyone.

'They're making for the ranch,' John said. 'I hope Trefina gets to that cave before they find her.'

'I hope so too, John,' Mike said quietly. 'Come on, we'll have to follow them. Keep a look-out in case they bushwhack us along the way.'

A slight smile appeared on Mike's lips. They had been riding away from Ringwald's men, now they were chasing after them.

★   ★   ★

Trefina was now in sight of the ranch. She could tell that the horse pulling the wagon had about had it. It had waited outside the saloon for a whole day and most of the night and had not been fed or watered. She knew the horse would not be able to pull the wagon up the hills to the cave. She would have to stop off at the ranch and see to the animal, then saddle up a fresh mount.

How she wished old Jake were there to help her. He would do it all far more quickly than she could. While she was at it, she attended to Mike's horse also. She contemplated saddling it up, but she knew she was not used to the animal, and it would be too big for her to handle easily.

She had just tightened the cinch on the saddle when she heard the sound of hoof beats. Were these men her father, Mike, Jake and Ben?

Trefina peered through the partly opened stable door. She counted six men. Her heart began to beat rapidly. She knew these men must be Ringwald's. What should she do? Hide here in the stable? Make a break for it for the hills? She knew the latter course would be futile, for they would follow her. If she had been able to reach there before they arrived she would have been safe, for they would not know of the secret cave.

'Spread out!' came an order from one of the men. Trefina guessed it must be Ringwald himself.

'It don't look as if anyone's at home, Mr Ringwald,' one of the riders said.

'No,' came the answer. 'We got here before them.' Then he noticed the wagon nearby.

'Or did we?' he added. 'Lightning took the wagon from outside the saloon, so he must have gotten here before us and let the others try and hold us off back there.'

'He must be inside,' another rider suggested.

'Maybe.' Ringwald nodded. 'Surround the house!'

The riders obeyed the command. Ringwald stayed at the front.

'Lightning!' he yelled. 'Come out now and you won't get hurt. If you're not outside in two minutes . . . '

Trefina's heart seemed to be pounding out of her breast.

Ringwald frowned when he received no reply from inside the house.

'Lightning! I'll give you one more chance. Come out now or you'll be burnt alive.'

Again, Ringwald received no reply.

'Right, you men, make some torches and burn the place down. He's had his chance.'

Trefina wished she had a weapon with her. She knew she could down a couple of them.

'Mr Ringwald,' one of the men began, 'mebbe he ain't in the house. He could be in the stable or barn — or even hidden by the trees at the side of the house — with his gun pointing straight at us.'

Ringwald visibly jumped at the man's words. He knew he could be right and he looked around him quickly, hoping to see a movement somewhere which would tell him where to fire.

'Come with me, Cassidy! We'll take a look in the stable first. Keep your eyes skinned for any movement. He's pretty handy with a gun, I've been told.'

Trefina swallowed hard. They were coming into the stable. She crouched down in a corner of one of the stalls, pulling some hay over her, but she knew she would not be entirely covered.

She could hear the men's movements in the darkness.

Ringwald motioned to Cassidy to light a lantern. He did so and the light from it cast shadows around the stable.

The men moved slowly, their fingers on the triggers, ready at the slightest sound.

Cassidy let off a bullet at a rustling sound in the far corner.

'It's only a rat, you fool!' Ringwald snarled.

The horses nickered in alarm at the sound. Ringwald wondered why Lightning had not fired at them in reply.

'Mr Ringwald!' Cassidy exclaimed. 'This horse is saddled, as if ready to go.'

'So it is.' Ringwald smiled.

They covered every inch of the place.

Then their footsteps stopped at the stall where Trefina was hiding. She felt herself trembling. Then Ringwald's words came to her.

'Well now, what have we got here?'

7

Trefina looked up at the faces of Ringwald and Cassidy. Cassidy was grinning broadly and Trefina felt foolish.

'I expected to find Lightning, not you, young lady,' said Ringwald. 'Where is he?'

'He'll be along,' Trefina answered.

'And we'll be waiting for him.' Ringwald's face looked grim. 'As for you . . . I have plans for you.'

Ringwald grabbed her arm and pulled her out of the stall. Mike Clancey's horse, Thunder nickered, knowing something was wrong.

'Why am I not seeing flames?' Ringwald shouted at his men.

'No!' Trefina cried out. 'Why are you doing this to us? It's not fair!'

Ringwald gave a short, harsh laugh.

'Maybe your father will see sense and

sign over the place to me. I intend having this ranch to join up with my own. I intend to own everything around here and he won't stand in my way any longer.'

Trefina tried to wriggle out of his grasp, but he held her more tightly.

'I see you've got a horse already saddled. Get on it, Miss Pickering! You're coming with me.'

Trefina hesitated for a second or two, but Ringwald pushed her towards the waiting horse.

She felt herself trembling as she mounted up. This was not supposed to happen. Mike was supposed to be their saviour, yet he was not on the scene. Where was he — and her father and the other two? Had they been killed by some of Ringwald's men?

Ringwald smiled as he saw the hurriedly made torches being thrown through the broken window. He took the reins of Trefina's horse and the two rode off, leaving his men to finish their task.

Mike Clancey and his two companions reached the ranch as Ringwald's men were riding off. Flames had taken hold and they knew it would not take long for the house to burn down.

'Mike, look!' John shouted in alarm. 'The wagon's outside. Trefina came here instead of going straight up to the cave. Could she be inside?'

Mike leapt off the mare and ran to the door.

'Use some pails of water from the trough — and hurry!'

'Trefina!' John screamed.

Mike covered his face with his arms as he entered the burning building. He looked around the downstairs rooms and began to cough as the smoke reached his throat. There was no sign of the girl and he ran up the stairs two at a time.

'Trefina!' Mike yelled, but there was no reply.

He went from room to room but it

was obvious she was not there.

He made his way downstairs again and was met by increasing flames. Several pails of water had been thrown inside the house. Mike pulled a thick cloth from the table and started beating with it at the flames around him. The curtains had started to burn and he beat at them frantically. It seemed as if this was only fanning the flames instead of putting them out.

Eventually, after what seemed like hours to them all, the conflagration had been extinguished.

Mike collapsed outside, coughing up the smoke from his lungs.

'Pour some water over me!' Mike's voice came out strained. His shirt was black and charred and the others noticed his arms had been burned.

The cold water which drenched his body felt good and comforting to Mike.

'Where is she?' John almost cried.

'One thing's for sure, she's not inside,' Mike answered. 'Take a look in the stable and barns. She could be hiding.'

While Ben and Jake went to look, John helped Mike to his feet and led him back inside the house. It looked a mess, but they could see that not too much damage had occurred: nothing that could not be put right.

John sat Mike down on a chair in another room which had not been damaged.

'I could do with Trefina here right now to attend to your arm. Where the devil is she? I'm worried, Mike,' John admitted.

Mike nodded. 'Me, too, John. You realize that if Ringwald has her, he'll use her as a hostage to get at you?'

Ben and Jake came into the house, worry showing plainly on their faces.

'No sign of Miss Trefina,' said Jake. 'Do you reckon she could have gone up to the cave?' he asked hopefully. 'One of the horses has gone.'

Mike looked up at John as he said,

'She'd need a horse if Ringwald took her.'

The room went silent, and after the heat shortly before, it felt suddenly cold.

★ ★ ★

Trefina was forced to hold on to the saddle pommel as Ringwald had the reins of her horse in his hands. They were alone as they rode towards his ranch and Ringwald's men did not catch up with them until a while later.

Cassidy, who seemed to be Ringwald's top hand, came up beside them. That same evil grin was still on his face. Trefina's heart beat in anger and loathing. How she wished she could knock that grin from his face. If only she had a gun to use on him and Ringwald. She felt tears of desperation come to her eyes, but what would be the use of crying? she asked herself sternly. No, she would not show these men that she was afraid of them. She would not give them the satisfaction of seeing her break.

They rode for the rest of the night and it was around six in the morning when they reached Ringwald's ranch house. She had never seen it before and noticed that it was no larger than their own place. She did not know whether he was married. No one had ever mentioned this fact. If he was married, then she pitied his wife. She could not imagine that he would treat her well as it was obvious that he liked to dominate.

They dismounted at the foot of the three steps leading up to the ornately carved door. This alone must have cost a pretty penny, she thought as she was led by the arm through it.

The furnishings looked expensive. What a waste if this opulence was only for Ringwald's benefit.

'Do you like it?' Ringwald asked her, indicating with a sweep of his arm around the large room.

'Why wouldn't I?' she answered tersely.

'You would fit in nicely here, I think.'

Trefina shook her head. 'I doubt it. This place might be full of expensive furnishings, but it has no heart — no soul. It's just a cold, dead place with a cold, dead man living in it.'

She saw the man's eyes narrow into a slit at her words. She could tell she had offended him, and she was glad.

Ringwald held her arm more tightly as he propelled her up the wide staircase. He opened one of the rooms and pushed her inside.

'I'll have some breakfast brought to you shortly. Don't try to escape, Miss Pickering, or I will be forced to kill you, and I don't want to do that. You are more use to me alive than dead.'

The door closed behind her and Trefina heard a key being turned in the lock.

She looked around her. The room was large and had a double bed. She felt it and found it was springy and looked comfortable. She crossed to the window and tried to open it but it was stuck fast. Even if she broke it, it was a long way down.

She realized there was no way of escape so she took off her boots and flopped down on to the bed. She yawned. It had been a busy night and she felt extremely tired. She thought about her father, Mike and the others for a while, then she was asleep.

★   ★   ★

After Mike's arms were attended to and they had rested for a while, Jake prepared breakfast for them all.

'We'll go up to the cave when we've finished,' said John. 'But I have a nasty feeling she won't be there.'

Mike nodded. 'Yeah, I think mebbe Ringwald's got her. And with all the men he has surrounding him, it'll be difficult to get her back. Will you give in and let him have this place, John?' Mike asked.

'I'll have to. Trefina means more to me than the ranch. She's my only link with her mother.'

Mike pursed his lips thoughtfully, and nodded.

'How long has your wife been gone?' Mike asked.

John thought for a moment.

'About ten years now. Trefina was only ten when she died. She caught a fever.'

'She was a fine woman, Mr John,' said Jake. 'A mighty fine woman. Beautiful, kind, gentle,' he added.

'Thank you, Jake.' John smiled slightly at his employee.

'Does Trefina favour her in looks?' Mike asked.

John shook his head.

'No,' he answered. 'She's as beautiful as her mother was, but Trefina's dark and Julia was fair.' John's next words came out quietly, as if saying them to himself.

'She don't look much like me, either.'

The others exchanged surreptitious glances.

'From her grandparents, no doubt,' Mike added.

'Yeah,' John nodded, grateful for his comments.

★ ★ ★

The four were soon riding towards the hills in search of Trefina, each with the feeling of futility at their actions. None of them really expected to find the girl up there, but they knew the search had to be done before moving off towards Ringwald's place.

Pickering led the way up the narrow pathway to the top of the rocky hill. It seemed to meander almost in circles at one stage and Mike felt sure he had passed one spot before, but John seemed confident he knew the way to the cave.

They came to it at last, but it was not visible to them from a distance. One pathway led in the opposite direction just before they came upon it. If someone had never been there before, they could easily have missed it and branched off in the wrong direction.

John dismounted first and tossed his horse's reins over some brushwood. He strode along and turned left behind a huge rock. Then it became clear that there was a cave ahead of them.

'Trefina!' John called out, hoping his daughter was inside. But no reply came to their ears.

8

The four went inside the cave and Pickering called his daughter's name again.

'Have you got a match, Jake?' he asked the old man.

'Sure, Mr John.'

Jake struck one on the wall of the cave and for a few seconds a tiny shaft of light shone. They quickly looked around them before the flame went out.

'This means we'll have to ride to the Ringwald place,' said Pickering.

'I don't like to think about the reception we'll get there,' Jake muttered under his breath.

'Mr Pickering,' Ben began, 'let me ride in first. If I can persuade some of them to come over to our side we might stand a better chance. Now the men who worked for you know what's happened to Miss Trefina, I reckon

73

they'll want to come back to you, like I have.'

'You could give it a try,' Mike put forward. 'But Ringwald might make you pay for changing sides. He wouldn't exactly welcome you on his property with open arms.'

'I know.' Ben nodded in the darkness. 'But I can't bear thinking of Miss Trefina in Ringwald's hands.'

The four made their way to their horses and mounted up. Once down the hill they headed northeast towards the Ringwald ranch.

★　★　★

Trefina awoke and daylight played through the curtained window. She sensed a presence in the room before she saw the man standing beside her bed looking down at her. It was Ringwald.

'Good morning, Miss Pickering. I trust you slept well?' he asked amiably.

She did not answer him and watched

as he put a breakfast-tray down on the dressing-table.

'Come and eat it while it's still hot,' he told her.

'I'm not hungry,' Trefina lied, and she realized she had not eaten since the morning before.

'Drink some coffee at least.' Ringwald smiled, but there was no warmth in his eyes. She noticed they were coal-black — like her own. How could she possibly have something in common with this monster standing before her?

Trefina's mouth was dry and she walked over to the dressing-table, pulled the stool nearer to it and sat down.

'Did you prepare it yourself?' she asked him.

He shook his head. 'No, I have a servant to do things like that for me.'

'I bet you do!' Trefina hissed.

She drank some coffee. It was good. She thought she might as well eat the food as it was there, and that, too, was very good and well-prepared.

Ringwald smiled down at her again.

'I'm sure you feel much better after that, Miss Pickering,' he declared. 'You're a very beautiful young woman. In fact, you're as beautiful as your mother was.' Frank Ringwald noticed the surprise on her face at his words.

'You knew my mother?' she asked him. She had never recalled seeing him at their ranch.

'Oh yes.' He smiled more broadly. 'I knew her all right.' He laughed, but it was a cold, mirthless laugh which sent a shiver down Trefina's spine.

'Now be a good girl and don't try to escape. No harm will come to you if you behave yourself,' he told her.

Ringwald took up her tray and left the room. She heard the key turn in the lock. What now? She wondered. What had happened back at her ranch house? Had her father and the others reached there in time to put out the flames? Had Ringwald's men killed them before they could do so? Oh! if only she knew what had happened.

A thought then occurred to her. If her father and his three men were now dead, then Ringwald would make her sign the Pickering ranch over to him, as it would be left to her on her father's death.

Tears suddenly came into Trefina's eyes. To think that her father might be dead was more than she could bear.

'Oh, Mike Clancey — Lightning — whatever your name is — please help us!' she cried out aloud.

★　★　★

It was around seven in the morning when the four arrived at the outskirts of the Ringwald ranch. They all stopped in unison. The ranch house could be seen in the distance through the tall, arched gateway. There were large letters in cast iron displayed in a semicircle above the gate. Even at this distance, the four knew that the letters read: RING-WALD.

'I'm gettin' mighty tired of seein'

Ringwald's name all over the place.'
Mike sighed.

Ben Haines smiled. 'Me, too.'

The cowboy looked at his three companions.

'What time is it? Anyone know?' he asked the three beside him.

Mike took out his familiar watch and looked at the dial.

'Seven,' he pronounced.

The three noticed the frown on Ben's forehead at this.

'We might be too late to catch the men in the bunkhouse. They'll have had breakfast by now and be out on the range. It'll be the round-up pretty soon. Then the cattle-drive to Wichita.'

'There'll be some men around I reckon,' said Mike. 'Ringwald wouldn't leave himself without bodyguards.'

Ben nodded at this, but added,

'They won't be former Pickering men though. Ringwald separated them into two groups — ex-Pickering and Ringwald's own men. We've gotta get hold of the riders you used to employ,

Mr Pickering, and talk to them.'

Mike nodded. 'You're right, Ben. But you're not going on your own. We'll all go.'

The four looked at each other and after a few seconds, each nodded in agreement.

They did not ride through the gateway, but turned left, following Ben as he led them in the direction of the range which by now was familiar to him.

'I'm surprised Ringwald separated his men into two factions,' said Mike as they rode. 'If they all worked together in one team, this would make it harder for any of your former riders to decide to return to you, John.'

'Yeah, you've got a point there, Mike,' John replied, nodding his head.

'Mebbe he's not as clever as he thinks he is,' said Jake.

'Let's hope not,' John added. 'The sooner we can get some backing behind us, the sooner we can get Trefina back. I just hope that insane monster hasn't harmed her at all.'

Cassidy sat on the top pole of the corral fence and inspected the horses. There was a particular white stallion he had his eye on. He intended having this one for his own. Where he sat he had a good vantage point of all around him and particularly the house. His thoughts went to the girl his boss had tucked away inside. Ringwald had said that he had plans for her. What sort of plans? Cassidy wondered. He would like the chance to fulfil plans he, himself, had in mind for her. A sly grin crossed his face at the thought of it. She was a beautiful young woman and he felt a stirring in his loins as he continued to think about her.

If only Ringwald would leave the house for a while. Then he would be free to pay the girl a visit.

After a while Cassidy jumped down from the fence and strode towards the house. He walked up the steps to the door and knocked on it.

A buxom black woman with a white apron around her ample hips opened the door.

'I want to see Mr Ringwald,' said Cassidy. The look of contempt for her was plain to see on his evil face.

'I'll get him for you,' the woman told him.

Cassidy did not wait to be invited in and entered through the open door into the hallway.

A few minutes later Frank Ringwald came up to him.

'What is it, Cassidy?' Ringwald asked with an edge of annoyance in his voice.

'I came to see what you want me to do for you today. I guess you'll want me and a few of the boys to hang around in case that Lightnin' fella and Pickering turn up?'

Ringwald nodded. 'If they've got the nerve.' He gave a short laugh.

Cassidy replied with a grin.

'Have you had any trouble with the girl?' he asked.

'No, she's been as good as gold. I

might even make her marry me. I've got no one to leave this place to when I go. I've left it a bit late for any children to inherit the ranch though, I reckon.'

Cassidy, as usual, sucked up to his employer.

'You're plenty young enough still, Mr Ringwald. Any woman would be mighty glad to bear your children' — he waved his arm in a semicircle — 'and get all this into the bargain.'

Ringwald smiled. This was just what he wanted to hear.

'The only trouble would be she might not co-operate. And you've got her old man to contend with,' Cassidy added.

'There are far more of us than there are of them,' Ringwald reminded him.

'When do you reckon they'll pay us a visit?' asked Cassidy.

Ringwald shook his head and shrugged his lean shoulders.

'Who knows. They're more than likely to try it under cover of darkness. Keep your eyes open, Cassidy, and tell the others to do the same.'

'Will do,' said Cassidy. He turned to leave, but not before he looked up the stairs to the landing where in one of the rooms was a beautiful young woman.

9

The cowboys were busy roping the calves and burning the Ringwald brand on to their hides. Pickering was wondering to himself how many of them originated from his own stock. Now that Ringwald had all his men working for him and had rustled the majority of his stock, Pickering knew that it really was not worth the trouble to carry on. No stock, no men, and no money coming in, plus the fact that his home would need a lot of attention to make it habitable again. Ringwald had taken everything from him — even his daughter.

Mike Clancey took a sideways glance at his new friend and could almost read the man's mind. There was sadness on his face, and defeat, but Mike could also see a spark of anger there which would keep the defeat from finally taking hold.

As they approached a group of the men, Ben Haines raised his hand in acknowledgement. One of the men went for his gun but Clancey's was already in his hand.

'We haven't come here for a fight,' Mike told them. 'We just want a word with you all.'

The man put away his gun and stood upright, waiting for Mike to speak again.

'You must all know by now that Ringwald is holding Miss Trefina Pickering hostage at his ranch house so that Mr Pickering will be forced to sell his place to him for her return.'

'I didn't know that,' said the man who had drawn his gun. He looked around at the hands working with him.

'Me neither,' said another.

'You've come to ask us to help you get her back?' another asked.

'We could do with your support,' Mike told him. 'The more, the better. The four of us could charge in alone, but we'd be shot down before we could reach Trefina. There's no telling what Ringwald will do with her — or has already done,' he added.

The men went quiet at this remark. They all had respect for John Pickering and his daughter, and secretly they felt ashamed at running out on them. But Ringwald's men were tough and would not hesitate to kill them if they helped to release Trefina from Ringwald's clutches.

'I don't know, Mr Pickering,' the first speaker began tentatively. 'We know Ringwald's gone too far this time, but . . . '

'I know.' Pickering nodded understandingly.

He turned to Mike and said, 'Come on, we're wasting our time here. We'll have to get her back by ourselves. It's no use trying to get help from these turncoats. We wouldn't be able to trust them if they did say they'd help us.'

Pickering's bitter words hammered home and the men now in Ringwald's employ felt uneasy and guilty.

The four riders turned their horses back in the direction of Ringwald's ranch house. Ben Haines turned in the saddle for one last look at his former friends. All the men were still looking at their retreating backs. He wondered what thoughts they had in their heads. As he turned back again he felt guilty at having joined the men in their betrayal before at last coming to his senses. He then realized that if it had not been for Trefina, he would probably still be with the men they were now leaving behind.

★   ★   ★

By now, Ringwald would have been halfway to the town that bore his name, had it not been for Trefina's presence in his house. He was sure Pickering and his three men would pay him a call at some time during the day — if not, at some time after dusk.

He went into the kitchen where his

black servant woman had just prepared a tray for Trefina.

The woman looked up at her employer and Ringwald knew what her thoughts were. He was under no illusions as to her feelings for him. Contempt, fear and loathing were three things Ringwald knew were simmering under the surface. He ignored this fact and knew she would not — dare not — betray him. He could trust her to do whatever he asked of her without any hesitancy.

Ringwald inspected the evening meal and nodded. 'She ought not to turn her pretty little nose up at this,' he said with a slight smile on his thin lips.

The woman did not reply and watched with a sullen expression on her face as her employer left the kitchen carrying the plate of food.

Trefina had been looking for some kind of weapon to use on the next person to enter the locked room. She had found nothing. She had looked in all the drawers and found them completely empty. As empty as the man himself, she thought. The only thing she could think of to use was a chair but found it too heavy to lift. It was sturdily built and the back was well-upholstered.

Trefina felt anger well up inside her again. She hated feeling so helpless and at Ringwald's mercy.

Then she heard the key turning in the door and saw it open. The smell of food came to her nostrils and it made her feel hungry.

Ringwald entered. He had a smile on his face.

Trefina was already standing and as he made his way to the dressing-table to put the plate down, Trefina rushed for the door and reached the landing before Ringwald came after her. She almost tumbled down the stairs as she headed for the front door but Ringwald soon reached her and pulled her round to face him. She felt his hand lash out across her face and a small cry of pain escaped her lips.

'That was very naughty, Trefina. Come back and eat your supper before it gets cold!'

Trefina felt herself being pulled by her arm up the stairs. He pushed her inside the door.

'Now eat your meal and don't try that again. You would not want me to become *really* angry.'

He locked the door behind him and she heard his footsteps fading away.

Trefina was shaking and her cheek hurt from the blow. Tears began to flow and all thoughts of food left her.

Cassidy was sitting on the front porch step when his employer strode out. By the look on his face, Cassidy guessed something had happened to upset the man.

'OK, boss?' Cassidy asked.

Ringwald did not answer the question but said, 'Keep your eyes open for Pickering and his men. Make sure the boys do the same. There are enough of you to stop them from trying to get the girl back, so I'm not too worried on that score. I'm going for a ride into the hills. I'll not be long.'

Ringwald breezed past Cassidy and made his way to the stables. A few moments later he rode off towards the hills at the back of the house.

Cassidy gave him a couple of minutes before he entered the house. He stood in the hall for a while and looked up the stairs. He should have enough time for what he had in mind, he reckoned.

As Cassidy climbed the stairs a thought occurred to him. Ringwald would have locked the girl in one of the rooms, making it impossible for him to get at her. He carried on nevertheless. Which room? he wondered. Then he saw a key in the keyhole of one of them. Ringwald had forgotten to take it with him when he left in such a hurry.

Ringwald's bodyguard turned the key in the lock and pushed the door open.

Trefina heard the key turning and guessed it was Ringwald coming back for the tray. Before her failed escape she had been very tempted by the smell of the cooked meal, but afterwards all thought of food left her.

When she looked at the man entering she found herself feeling even more afraid of him than Ringwald. The man named Cassidy had the same evil smile on his face.

He turned the key in the lock on the inside of the room and pocketed it.

'You and me are gonna get to know each other better,' he told her.

'Oh no we're not!' Trefina told him defiantly.

'Come on now, girl. You'll like it. I've never had no complaints before.'

'Maybe that's because the others weren't so particular — and they were getting paid for it.'

She could tell he did not like this statement. The smile vanished and he came up closer to her.

Trefina backed away, but there was not enough room to be able to keep out of his clutches. She found herself being scooped up and thrown down on to the bed. He was immediately on top of her and Trefina had not enough strength to hold him off.

★　★　★

Ringwald felt in his vest-pocket for a cheroot and a match and realized that he must have left the key in the lock after he had bundled the girl back into the bedroom. He continued to ride for a few seconds more. She should be safe there until he returned, he thought to himself. But then he remembered Cassidy. He knew the man would not be able to stop himself from trying to get at her.

Ringwald turned his horse back the way he had come. No one was going to have Trefina Pickering except himself.

10

Mike Clancey and his three companions drew up outside the gateway to the Ringwald ranch house. There were about six men in various positions outside the house and by the bunkhouse.

'They're Ringwald's men,' Ben informed them. 'His bodyguards.'

'Are there any more than six?' Mike asked.

'There are about ten out on the range, but these six keep close.'

Mike nudged Thunder's flanks with his heels and the four moved on towards the house.

The men came to a standing position as the four drew closer. Their guns were already in their hands. They looked a formidable bunch.

'Ringwald inside?' Mike asked them all.

He noticed them look at each other as if wondering what answer to give him.

'Mebbe,' said one of them who became their spokesman.

'Mebbe he is? or mebbe he ain't?' Mike replied.

'Depends,' said the spokesman.

Mike gave a deep sigh. 'Oh, get outa my way! I'll see for myself.'

He dismounted but his three friends stayed put.

The spokesman pulled back the hammer of his gun but found himself facing Mike's gun which had somehow miraculously appeared in his hand ready cocked. The spokesman and his fellow bodyguards stood with their mouths agape. Mike was quick to see one of them about to pull the trigger of his gun and Mike's own weapon barked out. The recipient of the bullet fell to the ground, clutching his arm.

The hammer of Mike's gun was cocked again and pointing directly at the spokesman.

'Do you wanna try?' he asked him. 'Throw down your gun! All of you do the same!'

The men did as they were commanded and allowed Mike to walk up the steps to the door and enter. His gun was still in his hand and ready. He looked around him but there was no sign of Ringwald.

Mike looked back at his friends and indicated with his head to follow him. He held his gun on the bodyguards who somehow did not seem at all willing to try any more shooting.

Just then Ringwald rode up in a cloud of dust. He drew his gun but Mike aimed his own and fired. The bullet just nicked the man's hand and he dropped his gun to the ground. Ringwald thought perhaps Lightning's aim was off and was surprised he was not dead beside his gun.

Ringwald looked around him at his so-called bodyguards with disgust.

'What the hell am I paying you all for?' he bellowed at them. 'What are you afraid of? He's only one man. You needn't worry about the other three.'

'I want my daughter, Ringwald. Bring her to me!'

Ringwald looked at John Pickering and a faint smile came to his lips. Pickering did not know it, but soon he was to become his father-in-law. It came to Ringwald at that moment why he had hurried back to the ranch house. There was no sign of Cassidy and he guessed where the man was. He hoped he was not too late.

'Hurry!' Ringwald told the four. 'I think one of my men might be . . . ' He trailed off and they all knew what he was saying.

Mike pushed Ringwald aside and leapt up the stairs two at a time. Ringwald hurried to the door where Trefina was inside. It was locked.

'Where's the key?' Pickering demanded.

'Cassidy!' Ringwald yelled. 'Open up this door at once!'

'Pa, is that you?' Trefina called out. 'Help me!'

Ringwald and Mike put their combined weight against the door and after a couple of thrusts, it burst open. Cassidy was in the process of getting up from the bed, and if it was possible for him, a guilty expression was on his face.

'Trefina. Has he . . . Has he . . . ?'

Trefina held her father to her.

'No, Pa. You all came just in time.' Her pent-up tears came freely now.

Everyone was preoccupied with Trefina and no one noticed Ringwald grab Cassidy's gun and fire it into the man's chest. Still holding the gun on the rest of them, Ringwald backed towards the open door.

'Trefina, come to me!' he told her.

'No. Never!' she told him.

'I'll kill your father if you don't come to me,' he said.

Clancey knew he could down the man easily, but they were all in a confined space and he did not want to hit anyone else.

Trefina left her father and walked up to Ringwald who grabbed her arm.

Ringwald backed out of the door with Trefina in front of him as a shield.

Trefina almost fell down the stairs as Ringwald pulled her along. They were soon out into the open and Ringwald's bodyguards crowded round them.

'Come on, follow me!' he yelled at them as he lifted Trefina up on to his horse. As he rode off with her in front of him, he fired a shot into the doorway. Ben Haines was hit, but not fatally.

'Take him inside and see to him, Jake,' said Mike. 'John, come on. We're going after them!'

As they rode, one or two of the bodyguards turned in the saddle and fired a couple of shots at Mike and John, but Mike's aim was straighter and two of them fell from their horses.

'That's two less to worry about,' he muttered to John.

Mike fired again and another fell to the ground.

'I'll be running out of ammunition at this rate,' he added.

Having Trefina in front of him, Ringwald was not gaining any speed. He was growing worried at seeing his men falling. It would not be long before there was only himself and Trefina. He guessed that Lightning would not shoot him in the back as the bullet might go through him into the girl. For as long as she was in front of him, he knew he would be safe.

★　★　★

Jake put his arm around Ben Haines's waist and half-dragged him into the house. The housekeeper came into the room and pointed to the couch.

'Put him down there and I'll see what I can do for him,' she said.

Jake looked into the woman's dark eyes and gave her a smile, which she returned.

'Thanks. I'm Jake,' he told her.

'I'm called Matilda, but people call me Tilda.'

She hurried away and brought back a bowl of hot water and some clean cloths. The bullet had gone through Ben's left shoulder which would save having to probe for it.

Soon the wound was washed and bandaged and already Ben's shoulder was feeling a lot better.

'Thanks, ma'am,' he said.

Tilda nodded in answer and returned with the bowl of bloody water to the kitchen.

Soon there came the sound of horses' hoofs outside. Jake looked out of the window to see the cowboys coming back for supper. They were the ones who had once worked for John Pickering.

Jake went out on to the front porch and watched as the cowboys dismounted outside the corral. He walked over to them.

They all recognized Jake and several of them frowned to see him standing there alone. Where was Pickering, Ben Haines and the man called Lightning? they wondered.

'Your boss has gone loco and rode off with Miss Trefina on the front of his horse,' Jake explained.

'Have Ringwald's bodyguards followed?' one of them asked him.

'Sure did, and Mike Clancey and Mr Pickering went straight after them. I reckon they'll head for town.'

The cowboys looked from one to another.

'How about it, boys? Do we lend Mr Pickering a hand?' They nodded.

'I reckon we should,' said another. 'Come on, boys, let's mount up. We're gonna pay the town of Ringwald an early visit. We'll make that apology for a sheriff do his duty.'

'Hold on a minute,' said Jake. 'Ben Haines was shot by Ringwald, but I guess he'll be OK in Tilda's hands. I'll let him know what's happening and I'll come with you.'

'OK, make it quick!' Bob Macey snapped.

Soon Jake and the ex-Pickering hands were heading for town at speed. They knew there would be gunfire ahead of them, but things had come to a head and had to be put right.

11

As Ringwald rode ahead of his few remaining bodyguards, Pickering and the man they called Lightning, he worked out what he was going to do. He would lock Trefina in a cell and use Bob Pyne the sheriff to keep her there. With his men behind him he could hold off Pickering's few retainers. He remembered that he had shot one of them — Ben Haines he thought his name was, so now there were only three of them to try to get Trefina back.

At last they reached town and Ringwald pulled Trefina from the saddle outside the sheriff's office. He fired a shot between two of his men but knew he had not killed Lighting or Pickering.

He held Trefina in such a way that her body protected his own as he pushed her into the office.

'What the devil's going on?' Pyne asked, getting up from his chair.

'Lock her up and keep your eyes on the door and window. Only let my men inside. No one else!' Ringwald commanded.

He turned to Charlie Cross, the deputy.

'Get those rifles ready!'

'You've no right to do this to me!' Trefina cried out. 'Take your hands off me! I've done nothing wrong. Why don't you arrest Ringwald? He's been holding me for ransom at his place so my pa will sign over his ranch to him. If you help him, then you are no better than he is and you'll face the consequences.'

Pyne looked hard at her face as he closed the cell door on her. He knew what she was saying was the truth. If the law outside the county got to know what was happening, then things could get messy. Pyne had not even been elected sheriff. Ringwald had put him in the sheriff's position so that he could do as he pleased. There was only one law around here, and that was Ringwald law.

Ringwald's men entered the office and the door was quickly shut behind them. Pickering and Lightning were close behind them.

'Barricade the door!' Ringwald ordered.

The sheriff's desk and a cabinet were hastily pulled across the doorway.

'That should hold them,' Pyne said.

'Yeah, but for how long?' one of Ringwald's men answered. 'We can't stay here for ever.'

'And they can't wait outside for ever either,' was Ringwald's reply.

Mike and John dismounted and tossed the reins of their horses over a hitch rail.

'We're not gonna get in there without trouble,' John commented.

'They'll have locked Trefina in the same cell they locked me in,' said Mike. 'I wonder if the hole's still in the wall, the one you all hoped I'd be able to squeeze through?'

John allowed himself a smile.

'That was expecting a lot. But Trefina's much smaller than you ... '

'Much,' Mike agreed. 'Keep your eyes on the front here. Let off a shot now and then so they think we're still around, and I'll go round the back and toss a rope down to Trefina.'

'OK, Mike. You can give it a try.'

As Clancey rode round to the back of the jail he pictured John, Trefina and Jake trying the same thing that he was about to do, only this time it was Trefina in the cell. The hole was still in the wall and Mike wasted no time in making a noose in the rope before throwing it up into the hole.

Trefina was sitting on a bunk when the rope came from above her and hit her on the head. She gave a small cry of surprise.

The men in the sheriff's office heard it. Ringwald rushed into the cell and took in what was about to happen.

'Oh no you don't, young woman,' he told her. He unlocked the cell door, grabbed at the rope and tied the end around the bars of the cell.

'Mike!' Trefina shouted up at the hole. 'Ringwald's found out. Get out of here quick!'

Clancey cursed under his breath. He would have to think of something else. He returned to the front of the sheriff's office where John was waiting for him. Mike could see the disappointment on the man's face at not seeing his daughter by his side.

Mike shook his head. 'They found out what I was doing,' he explained.

A bullet came from the office and past Mike's right ear. It was returned by Mike in an instant and he and John heard the scream from the recipient.

'I wonder who I hit?' Mike remarked.

'You can bet your bottom dollar it wasn't Ringwald,' John muttered.

'Mm.' Mike nodded. 'More's the pity.'

Men were beginning to come out on to the street to see what was going on. Mike wondered if this was a good thing or bad. Whose side would they be on? he wondered. If Ringwald's, then he and John would become sandwiched between two sets of enemies.

One man came up to the pair outside the office.

'What's going on?' he enquired. 'Who's holed up inside the jail?'

'Ringwald and some of his men and the sheriff,' Mike answered calmly. 'They've got Miss Trefina Pickering locked up in there. Ringwald's holding her hostage so's John Pickering will sell him his ranch.'

The man frowned and shook his head.

'Damn the man!' he growled. 'Pity someone can't put *him* in jail.'

'Do all the townsfolk think the same?' Mike asked him.

He shrugged. 'Most of 'em. He's run this county for years now — since his ol' man died. Anyone'd think he's a king or something the way he acts. We've needed some real law around here for a long time now.'

Quite a number of men had gathered outside the office by now. Mike's explanation of the events was passed from one to another.

Mike felt they were getting nowhere and something had to be done. He did not want anyone outside the sheriff's office hurt or killed, though.

'I reckon you all should keep away from the window. Ringwald ain't too perticular who he shoots,' Mike shouted out to the crowd.

They agreed and gathered in groups out of the firing-line each side of the window.

'Ringwald!' Mike yelled at the men inside the office. 'Send Miss Pickering out now! If she gets hurt in any way, I'll personally see to it that you hang.'

The reply was another bullet from the Ringwald faction.

'Who do you think you are, Lightning — the law?' Ringwald shouted back.

'I could be,' was Mike's reply. 'I might even be the President of the

United States for all I know.'

There was laughter all round at this. There were several voices in the crowd saying, 'The man's crazy,' or, 'Who is he, anyhow?' Only John Pickering knew that Mike's words could be true as far as he was concerned.

'You try and break in here, Lightning, and I'll kill the girl,' Ringwald shouted from within.

'What sense would that be?' Mike shouted back. 'Then you'd have no bargaining power and we certainly *would* break in.'

There was no answer from Ringwald this time. Mike was sure the man was thinking it over. At the moment there was stalemate.

'What are we gonna do, Mike?' John asked him.

Mike sighed. 'Nothin' fer the moment. We'll just have to be patient — and wait.'

They waited.

Half an hour later many horses' hoofs could be heard approaching the town.

Ringwald's cowboys charged up the street hollering and whooping. Some fired their guns into the air.

'They're the men who used to work for me,' said John.

'The question is — whose side are they on at the moment?' asked Mike. 'If they're for Ringwald, then we're sand-wiched between him and them.'

Mike's question was answered in the next few seconds as one of the men rode up to him and Pickering.

'We've come to help you, Mr Pickering.' The speaker was Bob Macey.

The man was thanked by a broad grin from Pickering.

'I'm much obliged, Macey. The trouble is, there's not a lot anyone can do at the moment. Ringwald threatened to kill Trefina if we burst in to get her.'

Macey thought for a few moments.

'OK. Best if we all get ourselves a drink — or two, then. They'll get hungry and thirsty after a while. They won't hold out for long.'

Pickering nodded. 'I don't care a

damn how long it takes, but Trefina will suffer too.'

Macey nodded. 'Sorry, Mr Pickering. Maybe one of us will come up with a plan after a few drinks.'

'There's Jake with them!' Pickering grinned.

Mike gave the man a wave of acknowledgement.

'Ben Haines is bein' taken care of by Ringwald's housekeeper,' Jake told them as he drew up.

'Macey, kill the man called Lightning!' It was Ringwald's voice from inside.

Macey turned his horse in a semicircle and fired into the now broken window of the sheriff's office.

'Kill him yourself, Ringwald. I quit.'

A bullet was fired from the office but Macey had moved off towards the saloon before it could hit him, followed by the rest of the cowboys.

Mike looked at John and frowned.

'I don't reckon they'll be much help to us, especially after they get a few beers inside them. They could end up shooting each other — or us.'

'I reckon their hearts are in the right place,' was Jake's opinion. 'They'll come through, I'm pretty sure of it.'

'Now we play the waiting game,' said Clancey.

12

'Hey, you in there! I need some coffee and something to eat!'

Ringwald turned from the window of the sheriff's office and looked in the direction from where the voice came.

'OK,' he shouted through to Trefina. 'We could all do with some.' He turned to the few men left to guard him. 'One of you go and get something for us to eat and drink from the cantina.'

'It'll need more than one of us to bring it all back here,' said Bob Pyne. 'That crowd out there might not let us through, anyhow.'

'You're the sheriff, aren't you? Take one of these men and do it!' Ringwald ordered.

Pyne slowly opened the door an inch.

'Two of us are coming out to bring food to those inside. You'd better let us through or . . . ' Pyne hesitated. 'Or Mr

Ringwald might hurt the girl.'

'He's making sure everyone knows the blame sits firmly on Ringwald's shoulders,' Mike muttered to his two companions. He turned to the crowd.

'Let them through,' he told them. 'We don't want anything to happen to Miss Pickering.'

The crowd pulled back to allow Pyne and another of Ringwald's men to walk along to the cantina down the street.

'They'll be even more jittery now,' said Mike. 'Keep them all focused on the front here and I'll try again to get to Trefina at the back. Don't watch me go. Keep your eyes on the window.'

John and Jake nodded. John fired a bullet inside just to remind them they were still there. It was returned but the men inside could not get an easy view of those standing to one side of the window.

Throwing a rope through the open hole into Trefina's cell had not been such a good idea, Mike realized. A ladder would be more useful. He thought for a moment and nudged Thunder's flanks with his heels and headed for the livery stables via the back way.

He dismounted outside the large closed door and dropped the reins to the ground. He knew that Thunder would not move again until he returned.

Mike pulled the door open wide and went into the dark stables. A lamp was hanging on a hook on a post and Mike lit it with a match. A smile came to his lips as he saw a ladder leading up to the hay-loft. It was more than ten feet long, Mike reckoned, and would be heavy to carry. Riding Thunder and dragging it along behind him would make it easier to get it to Trefina's cell. Mike noticed a coiled rope hanging up and he took it with him. His other one had been tied to the bars of the cell by Ringwald and he had had to leave it there.

After a bit of exertion, Mike fixed the ladder to the saddle cantle and within a few minutes he was at his destination.

Mike placed the ladder up against the wall. The top of it reached the hole. He knew he would have to attract Trefina's attention quietly and not startle her as before.

Mike climbed up the ladder and poked his head inside the hole.

'Trefina!' Mike whispered. 'Trefina, can you hear me?'

'Mike?' she called back, also in a whisper.

They had left her in the dark and they could not see each other, but gradually, Mike's outline appeared at the hole by the gentle light from the night sky.

Mike made a noose in one end of the rope.

'I'm throwing another rope down to you. Put it around your waist and hang on! I'll pull you up. Try walking up the wall as I do so, and keep quiet!'

Trefina pulled the noose over her head and tightened it slightly around her waist. She grabbed hold of the rope and tried her best to do as Mike had asked. At last she reached the hole.

Mike went down two or three rungs of the ladder to give Trefina room to swing her legs through the hole. He placed her feet on the rungs and guided her down.

Trefina could feel her heart beating faster. Having his body so close to her back and his arms protecting her from falling gave her a great feeling of relief. She felt even more relieved when they had both reached the ground.

She turned and found herself in his powerful arms. He could feel her trembling and he held her even closer.

'Thank you!' she whispered. 'I can't thank you enough.'

He gave her a gentle kiss on her forehead.

'I want to go home,' she told him quietly.

'Your home's in a mess. Ringwald nearly burnt the place down. We thought you were inside,' Mike explained.

'Did you go inside to find out?' Trefina gasped.

Mike nodded. 'Sure did. My arms got burnt a bit. But we were mighty relieved you weren't hurt.' He explained that they had gone into the hills to the cave to find her, then realized that Ringwald had her at his ranch.

'Where's Pa?' Trefina asked him.

'He and Jake are outside the sheriff's office keeping Ringwald and his men's attention at the front. The sheriff and another of Ringwald's men have gone to get some food and coffee.'

'I asked them for some,' said Trefina.

'Stay here in the shadows, Trefina,' Mike told her. 'I'm going back to your father to tell him you're safe. Now they haven't got you prisoner, we can go in blazing without fearing for your safety.'

Trefina watched as Mike walked back to her father and Jake. He left Thunder in her charge.

John Pickering looked at Mike with a frown.

'Where is she?' he asked.

'Back there keeping out of sight. She'll need a horse to get home.'

Pickering nodded. 'What are we gonna do about Ringwald?'

'I want to see him and his men behind bars. Then we'll have to give him a trial, I suppose. Is there a judge hereabouts?'

'No.' John shook his head. 'If we're gonna give him a trial, we'll have to get a circuit judge to come.'

'Is Miss Trefina OK, Mike?' Jake asked.

'Sure. She's a brave one.' Mike smiled.

He hesitated as if turning thoughts over in his mind.

'Jake, I want you to take Miss Trefina to the cave for safety. Put together some provisions and make sure she has water for a while. Let her have John's horse to ride, then come back here with it. With any luck those cowboys might come in useful to us.'

'Sure, Mike.' Jake grinned. 'I'll take real good care of Miss Trefina, don't you worry.'

Jake mounted his own horse and led

Pickering's down the street towards the place where Mike had left Trefina.

'Here comes the sheriff and the other man with the coffee and food,' said Pickering. He nudged Mike's arm.

'On no account must they go back in there,' said Mike.

John looked at his friend and frowned.

'What's your plan, Mike?'

'I want to hold out for as long as possible before Ringwald finds out that Trefina has gone. If they go back in there and go to give her some coffee, they'll know they haven't got her to bargain with.'

John nodded.

The sheriff and the other man had come to the sheriff's office by now. They looked expectantly at Mike and John.

'Both of you, sit down here!' Mike ordered, pointing to the wall of the office at the side of the window.

'But we've gotta take this inside,' said Pyne.

'You've gotta do no such thing,' Mike replied. 'You'll do what *I* tell you. Didn't you bring any mugs for the coffee?' he asked, noting their absence.

'There's a couple inside,' Pyne explained.

'That's no good to me!' Mike bellowed. He gave a long sigh then turned to John.

'We'll have to drink it from the coffee-pot I guess.'

John grinned. 'It'll be a bit hot.'

Mike shook his head and took the coffee-pot from Pyne's hands. He put it carefully to his lips and took a sip.

'Mm. It needs some sweetening. I've a damn good mind to send you back and get some more to my liking, Mister Sheriff.'

John laughed at the bewildered expression on Pyne's face. The tables seemed to be turning at the moment.

'Lightning!' The voice came from inside the office. 'Send Pyne and Johnson in here at once with that food and coffee!'

'Sorry, Ringwald!' Mike shouted back. 'There might not be enough left after we've had our fill.'

'Send it in at once!' Ringwald's shrill voice came back. 'Pickering, your daughter needs some food and coffee. Tell that Lightning feller to let the sheriff and Johnson through.'

Mike shook his head vigorously at John so he would not let it slip that Trefina was no longer in the cell.

'I'm sure my daughter will survive a bit longer. She's a tough girl.'

'Let the food and drink through. Now!' Ringwald ordered again.

'Now, let's see what we've got wrapped up in this paper,' said Mike as he took the parcel from Johnson and opened it up. 'Ah, tortillas! They'll do to fill a gap. Here, John. Take one. Roll it up, it'll be easier to eat that way.'

The crowd that had gathered were edging forward. The aroma was making them all feel hungry. They realized that there would not be enough for them all.

When John and Mike had eaten their

fill and drunk most of the coffee, Ringwald's voice rang out once more.

'Don't finish it all! Bring the rest in here!'

Mike shook his head and frowned.

'Did you hear something, John? I could have sworn I heard a coyote — or was it a rattlesnake? It couldn't have been a man, surely. I don't reckon there are any real men in that jailhouse.'

'What are you gonna do, mister?' one of the crowd called out. 'Are you gonna kill him?'

'Is that what you'd all like me to do?' Mike called back.

'Yeah!' came the reply. 'Kill him! Kill him! Kill him!'

13

The chanting of the crowd for his blood made Ringwald very uneasy. He knew he was comparatively safe where he was with his men around him and the girl safely locked up, but he knew he had never been popular with the townspeople. They only kept quiet out of fear. If any one of them had spoken out of turn, one of his men had been swift to shut them up. On one or two occasions it had been permanently.

Bob Pyne, the sheriff, hated his guts, he was well aware of that, but Pyne had a family to think of and Ringwald knew he would never do anything to jeopardize their safety. Nevertheless, this Lightning character had drawn the people together against him and Ringwald was worried. More worried than he cared to admit.

'You wouldn't dare to try and kill me,

Lightning. You don't want to risk harming the girl, do you?'

'No, Ringwald, you know I'd never do that,' Mike shouted in reply. 'You can stew for all I care. Sooner or later you'll be begging me to let you come out.'

'Don't be a fool!' came back the reply. 'The girl can't survive too long without food and water.'

'Mr Pickering is willing to wait. We'll give you until morning before we come in, guns blazing.'

Ringwald ground his teeth together. His men were looking intently at him. They could see he was becoming edgy and none too confident.

'What are we gonna do, boss?' Reg Pretty asked him.

'Wait, of course! No one's gonna get the better of me. We're quite safe in here while we've got the girl,' Ringwald assured him.

'I only hope you're right.' Pretty shrugged his thin shoulders.

Suddenly there was a whooping and hollering from the cowboys who had drunk their fill at the saloon. A couple of shots were fired into the air and several of the crowd decided it was best to go home to bed and leave the two factions to fight it out without them.

'We're back, Mr Pickering,' Bob Macey, one of the cowboys, said unnecessarily.

'Yes, Macey.' Pickering nodded and smiled. 'We're quite aware of that.'

'What do you want us to do?' Macey asked eagerly, like a schoolboy of his teacher.

'Keep an eye on this place and don't let anyone in or out. I reckon Mr Clancey here and I need a break. Can I trust you to do that for me?'

'Sure thing, Mr Pickering,' Macey replied.

'Thanks. We appreciate it. Very much indeed. We won't be long.'

Macey dismounted. His friends did likewise and they sat on the boardwalk outside the sheriff's office.

Mike turned to John and said quietly, 'I'd best get that ladder returned to the livery stable so no one will know that Trefina's been busted outa jail. I'll meet you in the saloon in a few minutes.'

The two friends walked away in opposite directions. Mike returned the ladder using Thunder to drag it as before. As he was already there, Mike decided to leave his mount in one of the stalls and give him a feed while he was at it.

He had no idea how long this stand-off outside the sheriff's office would take, but as long as Trefina was now safe, he was not too much bothered.

The saloon was filling up again as the bystanders to the skirmish outside the sheriff's office began to return. They were certain that not much would happen for a while and guessed both sides would get bored with the dragging out of events.

John Pickering was already sitting at one of the tables and had bought Mike a beer.

'I feel a darn sight easier now I know

Trefina's out of harm's way,' said John.

'When Jake returns we'll know she's OK, then we can rush the jailhouse without any fear for her.'

John nodded and studied his friend's face. He was a good-looking young man, he thought to himself. He couldn't be more than about twenty-eight or so, he reckoned. His shock of straw-coloured hair protruded from under his hat, over his forehead. His eyes were blue with lines at the corners through squinting in the sun. If Mike Clancey were to grow fond of Trefina, then he knew he would be only too happy for her to marry him. Somehow, though, he had a deep feeling inside him that Mike Clancey would never put down roots anywhere. He would need to travel the country in search of his identity.

★　★　★

As Trefina and Jake reached the Pickering ranch house, Trefina's heart sank. Mike had warned her that the place was quite badly burned, but seeing it for herself made her accept it.

'Quite a mess, Miss Trefina,' said Jake as he dismounted outside the house.

'It most certainly is,' Trefina responded. 'Will we ever be able to put it right again?'

'It'll need some hard work on it, but it should come right.'

Jake came round to the left side of her father's horse which she had been riding and helped her down.

'If something's not done about Ringwald, we might be wasting our time making this place habitable again.'

Old Jake shook his head and smiled. 'Now don't you worry, Miss Trefina. That Lightning feller and your father will put things right. The cowhands who used to work for us have come back on our side, so things are looking a bit brighter.'

Trefina walked ahead of the old man and hesitated on the threshold.

'I most certainly hope you're right,

Jake. Come on, let's put some food and water together. Do we have any food?' she asked him as she stepped through the black ash on the floor.

'The fire didn't touch the kitchen, but there wasn't all that much left. Don't forget we never replaced the stuff Ringwald's men spoilt.'

Trefina picked her way towards the kitchen and was pleased that Jake was right. She realized that the food could be contaminated by smoke, but she hoped it wouldn't matter too much. If all went well she would not have to stay up there in the cave for too long.

Trefina made Jake and herself a cheese sandwich to eat immediately before they set off. She turned up her little freckled nose.

'It's a bit dry,' she said.

'At least it will fill a hole.' Jake grinned.

Trefina put what was left in a hessian bag and found three canteens which she filled from the pump outside.

'OK.' She nodded. 'Let's ride.'

They rode for an hour towards the hills, but neither of them had noticed a rider following them.

The pathway up the hillside was narrow and at times steep, but Trefina had used it before and remembered the pitfalls and the concealed path that could so easily be missed.

At last they turned left. It was six o'clock in the morning and everything felt fresh and cool, but they knew that within an hour it would be hot and dusty again.

'Will you be OK on your own, Miss Trefina?' Jake asked her solicitously.

'I guess so,' she answered with little conviction. 'So long as no one knows I'm here, I should be safe enough.'

Jake turned to go, leaving Trefina at the entrance to the cave.

'Jake,' she began, 'from now on I'm no longer *Miss* Trefina. I've known you long enough now and you're more than an employee of my pa's — you're a good friend and I trust you with my life. I'm now just Trefina.'

Jake nodded. 'OK Miss — er — Trefina.' He laughed at not being able to get out of the habit.

Jake then turned sharply at the sound of a horse's hoofs nearby. He drew his .45 as a rider came up beside them.

'Oh!' Trefina exclaimed. 'It's you.'

14

'Hold on there, Jake! Don't shoot me! I've already got one gunshot wound.'

Jake and Trefina looked up at the rider and sighed with relief.

'Ben Haines! Are you fit to ride just yet, boy?' Jake demanded to know.

Ben dismounted and dropped the reins to the ground.

'Wal, at least I wasn't shot in the leg or somewhere else nearer the saddle.' He grinned broadly. 'What's been happening?' he asked them.

Trefina related what had happened to her after Ringwald rode off with her in front of him in the saddle.

'Mike Clancey found a ladder and tossed a rope down to me in the cell and pulled me up. And here I am!'

'So what's the score? Where's Ringwald now?' Ben asked.

'Him and what's left of his men are

barricaded inside the sheriff's office. When Trefina an' me left the town, Ringwald had no idea that she was no longer in the cell. As soon as I get back to town to tell them that she's safe, they'll break in and get them. Oh, by the way,' Jake added as an afterthought, 'the men who used to work for Mr Pickering now work for him again.'

'That's great!' Ben exclaimed.

'Are you coming with me, Ben?' Jake asked him.

Ben took a long, lingering look at Trefina.

'Wal, I kinda thought I'd stay here and take care of Miss Trefina until you come back. I won't be much good to any of you with my arm in a sling,' Ben explained.

'Hm,' Jake muttered. 'I don't know about that. How do I know you won't follow me back to town and let Ringwald know where Trefina's hiding?'

Ben sighed. 'Jake, you must know by now that I wouldn't do a thing like that.

I've finished with Ringwald. Like the rest of the boys, I wish I'd never left Mr Pickering. I promise I'll take care of Miss Trefina. I won't lay a finger on her. That's God's honest truth.'

Jake looked at Trefina to see what she thought of it.

'I suppose it'll be OK,' she said without any real conviction in her voice. After thinking it over for a moment or two longer, she nodded.

'I'm sure I can trust Ben,' she said. 'Go on, Jake, get back to town. Pa and Mike can then stop worrying about me.'

Jake mounted up and looked down at the two left behind in the entrance to the cave.

'I've gotta take Mr John's horse back to him. I'll bring you one when we come for you. Goodbye, you two.'

They waved him off and watched until he was out of sight round the bend of the path.

★　★　★

The cowboys who had changed allegiance back to John Pickering were milling around on their horses. They were becoming bored and were fired up for action which did not seem to be happening.

'You out there!' came the ringing voice of Ringwald. 'We're still waiting for food and coffee. Miss Pickering must be very thirsty by now.'

'Come on out and get it!' Mike shouted back. 'We've got a big reception committee waiting to see you.'

'Do as I say!' Ringwald's voice rose an octave. 'While I've got Miss Pickering, you won't do anything stupid. Now bring us that coffee at least.'

'Sorry, Ringwald,' said Mike. ''Fraid it's all been drunk.' Mike picked up the pot of coffee and tipped it up until the rest of the liquid dripped into the dusty road. 'There, did you see that?' he asked.

A bullet whistled past Mike's ear from inside the office.

'Ringwald!' Mike shouted. 'Someone in there's a rotten shot. You'll be run out of ammunition pretty soon I reckon. You might just as well come on out with your hands held high. The sheriff's out here ready to arrest you all — ain't you, Sheriff?' Mike turned to the once brave lawman who'd had Ringwald's backing.

Ringwald was silent, until they heard expletives being screamed.

Mike grinned. He guessed that Ringwald had now found that the cell he expected Trefina to be in was empty.

'Where is she?' Ringwald yelled.

'Where you can't get at her, Ringwald. Now, will you come out before we come in?'

There was a brief silence, then Ringwald shouted, 'Come in and get me! We're waiting for you, Lightning. We're not out of shells yet.'

Mike knew that if he tried pushing at the door with his body, those inside would shoot at him through the door. One bullet at least would be sure to find its mark. At the same time, if those outside the door were to fire at it in unison, bullets would hit some of them. He guessed that Ringwald would push his men in front of him to bear the brunt of the bullets. There were more of them on the outside, and in time Ringwald's men would be whittled down to none.

'You men inside! You know you'll be killed one way or another. Come out and give yourselves up and you'll get a fair trial. Stay with Ringwald and you won't be alive to get a trial.'

'OK, Lightning!' one of the men shouted. 'I'm coming out. Don't shoot!'

The door opened slightly and they heard a gunshot, then a scream. They guessed what had happened. Ringwald had shot the man in the back for deserting him.

'Now mebbe you'll realize what kind of a man you're following. What are you gonna do about it?'

The men outside the office could not see what was happening inside, but after a few moments one of them spoke up.

'Ringwald's gun has been taken away from him. We've got our guns on him and we're coming out. Ringwald will be at the front.'

Mike and John exchanged glances. Was this a trap? The guns in the men's hands were held steady. Their eyes were fixed on the door.

Mike used his hand to tell the men to keep out of the line of fire when Ringwald came out. They moved to each side of the door and waited.

At last the door began to open.

'Hold your fire, Lightning! We're coming out. We're giving ourselves up. Ringwald is coming out first.'

The door opened wider and then wider still. Ringwald appeared in the doorway and he was not carrying a gun. He looked angry and even a little scared. He was not used to obeying orders, only to giving them. It suddenly made him feel small.

'Good day to you, Mr Ringwald.'

Mike grinned. 'You don't look particularly happy.'

Mike indicated to the cowboys nearest Ringwald's men to relieve them of their weapons.

'What do we do with 'em now, Lightning?' Macey asked, his face beaming.

'We march them back in again,' Mike replied. 'Into the cell and lock it after them. And then, if they behave themselves, we might give them some coffee and something to eat. Nothing too fancy, mind.'

The cowboys jeered and laughed at this. Most of them dismounted from their horses and all tried to get into the sheriff's office at once to do as Mike had told them.

''Fraid it's a bit cramped in there, Mr Ringwald.' Macey grinned again. 'The cell was only made for two at the most.'

'You're making a big mistake, Macey,' Ringwald told him. 'Who's going to pay you now? What about my cattle? Who's going to drive them to Wichita?'

Macey shook his head and shrugged his shoulders.

'We could take them, and Mr Pickering's, too — those he has left, of course. Then Mr Pickering will get half of the proceeds. After all, Mr Ringwald, half of his cows somehow got mixed in with yours, didn't they?'

Ringwald frowned. 'OK. I haven't got much choice, have I?'

Macey shook his head. 'No, not much. You agree to that, do you?' he asked.

Ringwald nodded.

'Is that a definite 'yes'?'

'Yes,' Ringwald said grudgingly.

John Pickering came up to the bars of the cell and looked long and hard at his adversary.

'Who's your next of kin, Ringwald?'

Ringwald looked surprised at the question.

'I haven't anyone,' he admitted reluctantly.

'Yes you have,' Pickering answered him.

'I've got no brothers or sisters and I've never had children. Not that it's any of your business, Pickering. If you must know, I intended marrying your daughter so she'd give me children to leave the spread to.'

'Marrying Trefina would be illegal,' John told him.

Ringwald gave a laugh of derision. 'It might have been against her will, and yours, too, but it could hardly be called illegal.'

'Well that's where you're wrong, Ringwald. It's very much my business.'

Ringwald frowned again. 'How come?'

'You have a daughter.'

Ringwald gave a harsh laugh. 'How the devil are you going to prove that?'

'I was told by her mother.'

'Who was that? Some saloon girl?' Ringwald moved around the small amount of floor space available to him and looked anxious and slightly worried.

'No,' John answered quietly. 'Someone much finer than a woman whom you'd paid for it.'

'I tell you I have no daughter!' Ringwald's voice rose slightly.

John's chest was visibly heaving. Mike noticed the man's teeth were grinding together in anger and sorrow.

'The woman who told me,' he said slowly, his voice becoming husky, 'was my wife.'

15

The room was hushed. There were many open mouths at John Pickering's statement.

Ringwald frowned and shook his head.

'Are you suggesting that I'm Trefina's father?' he asked.

'I'm not suggesting it, Ringwald, I'm telling you. Do you deny that you came to my house while I was in town and . . . took my wife . . . raped her, to put it bluntly.'

Ringwald did not reply.

'What's wrong, Ringwald? Are you feeling ashamed of yourself all of a sudden, after all this time?'

'Your wife was lying,' said Ringwald.

'I hardly think so. When I came home that night, she was crying. She cried quite a bit after that. She wouldn't say what had happened, but when she began to show, well I guessed I might not be the father. It was only on her death-bed that she told me what happened. How it happened.'

Ringwald laughed. 'And you did nothing about it, did you? You're not much of a man, are you, Pickering.'

'Maybe not. I'm not a brave man, I admit that. But if I had come gunning for you and killed you, I would have been put away or hanged. Then who would have taken care of Trefina? For all my lack of bravery, I reckon I'm the better man. To enter a man's home and rape his wife . . . what kind of a man does that make you? You're no better than an animal, and that's an insult to an animal.'

Ringwald threw back his head and laughed. It felt good to see the strain on Pickering's face.

John went for his gun but Mike slapped it down.

'Don't waste a bullet on him, John. Let the law deal with him. There ain't many folks around here who'll put in a good word for him.'

John nodded and reholstered his gun.

'I guess you're right, Mike.' He turned to leave the room.

'Where's the darned key to the cell?' he asked of anyone who might know.

'Here it is, Mr Pickering,' said Macey, handing it to him.

'This is staying with me until they stand trial. They can be fed through the bars — like you'd feed animals.'

Mike followed John outside. John breathed in the early-morning air in an attempt to get the smell of evil from his nostrils from the men locked in the cell.

John Pickering was visibly upset at his revelations. He felt he had somehow besmirched Julia's memory by revealing what had happened to her twenty years ago.

Mike put his hand on his friend's shoulder.

'Come on, John. Let's find a room for what's left of the night and rest up some.'

John nodded and walked beside the tall young man who had become such a good friend over the past few days.

★ ★ ★

When Jake left Trefina with Ben Haines, she felt slightly ill at ease. Ben had shown that he was on the Pickering side against Ringwald, but she hardly knew the young man. Her instincts told her that Haines thought a lot of her. She hoped she could trust him to keep any feelings for her he might have to himself. She doubted he would attempt anything with her with his arm in a sling. She could tell he was in some pain.

'Ben, shouldn't you go into town and see a doctor for that shoulder of yours?' she asked him.

'I'll go later,' he said. 'That house-keeper of Ringwald's seemed to know what she was doing. I reckon she tended to it as good as any doctor.'

Trefina put her hands in the pockets

of her divided skirt and walked around the cave. Ben could tell she did not feel at ease with him there.

'I wonder how long we've got to stay here?' she asked.

Ben shrugged his shoulders, then winced at the pain.

'Your pa will come for you soon enough I reckon. I wouldn't mind betting Ringwald and his men are locked up in the jail right now.'

'Do you really think so?' she asked. 'I do so hope Pa and Mike are safe. Mike rescued me from the cell by using a ladder. I'm so glad he came along when Ringwald's men stopped the wagon and wrecked the provisions. He's like a knight in shining armour.'

Ben noticed her face was almost glowing at the thought of the man some called Lightning. He realized he was feeling a bit jealous of him at that moment. After all, it had been Ben himself who had released Clancey from the jail. Ben nodded grudgingly.

'I guess he's a straight kinda feller.

I'd rather be on his side than against him.'

Trefina smiled broadly.

'I wonder if he's married?' she said quietly, as if to herself. 'He doesn't even know who he really is and that picture of a woman inside his watch could be his wife.'

'The watch could have been his father's. The woman might even be his mother.'

Trefina's mouth opened in surprise.

'Oh yes! You could be right, Ben.'

It was the first time she had used his name and he liked to hear her voice saying it. If only she would forget Lightning and concentrate on him.

★　★　★

Jake reached town around noon. He wondered where he would find John Pickering and Mike Clancey. There was no one hanging around the sheriff's office. He wondered what could have happened in his absence. Had John and

Mike turned the tables on those inside? Was everyone still alive, or had they killed each other during the night?

Jake tossed the reins of John Pickering's horse over the hitch rail, then dismounted and did the same with his own mount's reins. He walked slowly up to the boardwalk and peeped in at the window. Macey and a few of the cowboys were lounging around in there. There was no sign of Ringwald and his men.

Jake looked up and down the street. There was no sign of John or Mike. He decided to ask inside the sheriff's office.

When Jake entered, the cowboys looked up sharply. Their facial features relaxed when they saw it was Jake.

'Where's Mr John and Mike?' he asked.

'Having something to eat at the cantina,' Macey told him. 'We're taking it in turns. Someone's gotta keep an eye on Ringwald and his men in the cell. It's a mite cramped in there.' He laughed.

Jake gave a sigh of relief. 'Thank the good Lord it's worked out right,' he said.

'Jake,' Macey began hesitantly, 'did you know that Ringwald had John Pickering's wife and Trefina is Ringwald's daughter and not John's?'

Jake gave a gasp at the revelation. 'No! No it can't be true. And yet . . . '

'You'd guessed?' asked Macey.

'No, I never did. But it makes sense. Miss Trefina looks more like Ringwald than Mr John. You mustn't speak about it any more, do you hear me?' Jake demanded. 'You must never mention it again.'

Jake was breathing heavily and he felt his heart was breaking.

He left the office hurriedly and rode down the street to the cantina, leading John Pickering's horse, where he found his two friends just finishing their meal.

'Jake!' John Pickering exclaimed in obvious pleasure at seeing the man. 'Come and have some food.'

Jake sat down beside them and John

hailed the waiter over again.

Within ten minutes a spicy meat-dish was placed before him, together with a mug of coffee.

John looked hard at his old employee and wondered if he'd heard about what had gone on in the jail. Jake sensed he was being scrutinized and looked up into John's grey eyes.

'You must have spoken to someone to know where we were,' said John.

'I called in at the sheriff's office and Macey told me.' Jake shovelled in a forkful of food and munched slowly, waiting for John to ask him what else he had found out. When further questions did not come, Jake continued.

'I know about Miss Trefina,' he told him. 'It's a shame everyone had to know, Mr John. A real shame.'

John nodded sadly. 'I know, Jake. I've kept the secret from the day Julia died. I didn't want Trefina to know who her real father was, and how it came about. I'm not sure I ought to tell her now. But there is something I need to do that will ensure she'll inherit Ringwald's businesses. She deserves to have it all when he's gone. After all, before he found out she was his daughter, he did say he intended marrying her to get an heir to his property.'

Jake's mouth stayed open with a forkful of food mid-way to it.

Mike broke the silence by saying, 'You'd best find yourself a lawyer and get Ringwald to write Trefina into his will or whatever else needs to be done to make it legal.'

'You're right,' John nodded. 'But there's only one lawyer in town, and you can bet your bottom dollar he's in Ringwald's pocket. He might refuse to take me on as a client.'

'At the moment,' Mike began, 'Ringwald's in no position to have anyone in his pocket, but you are. In your pocket you have the key to Ringwald's cell.'

16

'What is Mr Ringwald in jail for?' Thomas Ladd, attorney-at-law asked John as he, Mike and Jake sat down before him at his desk.

'Just about everything,' said John.

'I can't force him to make a will in favour of your . . . his daughter,' Ladd explained.

'Even though he was gonna force me to sell him my ranch?' John exclaimed in disgust. 'He not only terrorized us and tried to burn my house down, he then abducted my daughter to make me sell it, and you tell me that you can't force him to make a will in favour of his own daughter?'

'Ah.' Ladd raised a forefinger in the air as if to make his words seem very legal. 'But you can't prove your daughter is now Ringwald's daughter, can you?'

John breathed deeply, then said, 'My wife would hardly tell me a lie on her death-bed. Ringwald raped her and she bore a child. Somehow Julia and I couldn't seem to have children together, and we didn't have any after Trefina was born. If you look closely at Ringwald and Trefina, you'll see certain characteristics which will give credence to what I've said.'

Ladd nodded sagely. 'I'll need a retainer.'

'How much?' John asked, raising an eyebrow.

'Er, shall we say thirty dollars?'

'OK,' John replied, 'but I want results — in *my* favour, not Ringwald's. He'll need a lawyer when his trial comes up and as you're the only one in town, you'd better send for another for him.'

'Yes,' Ladd said. 'I'll see there's one here when the circuit judge arrives — in about two weeks, I think.'

John stood up and his two companions did likewise.

'Well, are you coming to the jail to

sort this will out?' he asked the lawyer.

'He's in there with other prisoners, I heard. I can't conduct legal business like that. Bring him to my office and I'll make some notes as to what holdings he has.'

John ground his teeth together in anger.

'That man's not leaving the jail until the day of his trial,' he said emphatically.

Ladd shrugged his shoulders.

'He either comes here or I'll return your retainer. What is it to be, Mr Pickering?'

'We could handcuff him,' Mike suggested. 'He won't have a gun so I doubt we'll have any trouble from him.'

John sighed dejectedly. 'Oh, all right. If you two help me guard him on his way here, then I guess we'll manage OK.'

John led the way out of the lawyer's office. Mike was last to leave.

'See you in a bit then, Mr Ladd.'

The lawyer nodded. But Mike did

not like the look in the man's eyes. There was something about him that made Mike feel he could not entirely trust him. He hoped his feeling was not justified.

'Was Trefina OK when you left her in the hills?' John asked Jake.

'Sure. Ben Haines turned up. He followed us up to the cave and I left him there with her for company,' Jake told him.

John stopped suddenly in the street and pulled Jake around to face him.

'What?' he demanded. 'How could you have been so damn stupid? What if he . . . touches her?'

Jake stood his ground.

'Now hold on there, Mr John! Ben's recovering from a gunshot wound and is in no condition to do much at all. He wouldn't hurt Miss Trefina, I know he wouldn't. I'm sure she'll feel a lot better with him for company than being up there on her own.'

Pickering lowered his eyes away from Jake's direct look.

'I'm sorry, Jake. I should have trusted your judgement. I know you'd never leave Trefina in a position of any danger.' John held out his hand to the old man and Jake took it immediately.

Macey and some of his friends were still lounging around the sheriff's office when the three walked in.

'Where's the sheriff?' Mike asked them. 'I'd clean forgot about him. Maybe he ought to be in that cell with the rest of them.'

'He's gone off home to his wife and kids,' Macey told them. 'He weren't to blame for working for Ringwald. His family were threatened, after all.'

Mike nodded. 'Yeah, I guess you're right. We're taking Ringwald to the lawyer. Ringwald is gonna make his will.'

Macey and one or two others laughed at this.

'I guess you'll make sure that a certain young lady will get a big inheritance, eh, Mr Pickering?'

Pickering shot Macey a savage glance.

'Who else will he leave everything to? Trefina deserves it after the way she came into the world.'

Macey nodded, the grin still on his face. 'Quite so, Mr Pickering. Quite so.' He followed John, Mike and Jake into the jail.

Mike drew his gun and Jake and Macey followed suit while John unlocked the cell door.

'Come on, Ringwald! We're going for little walk down the street. Get back, the rest of you! Try any funny business and you won't live to regret it.'

Ringwald walked out of the cell and Macey handcuffed him. The rancher felt ill at ease without his men for backing. What had Pickering in mind for him? He felt sure he would not kill him or he would be charged with murder.

'Where are you taking me?' Ringwald asked as they left the sheriff's office.

'We'll let it be a little surprise,' replied John. He was feeling rather pleased with himself at the moment. He hoped this feeling would last.

When they stopped outside Thomas Ladd's office, Ringwald frowned and looked at his adversary.

'What's this, Pickering?' he demanded.

'I reckon it's time you made out your will,' Pickering replied.

'Oh, I get it. I leave everything to the woman you call my daughter, and then what happens to me? I have a fatal accident or something?'

Mike laughed. 'We hadn't thought of that, had we, John? You know, that's not such a bad idea. Now let me see . . . What kind of an accident might happen to you?'

John smiled at Mike's levity.

'He could be sitting comfortably in an armchair at home and suddenly his house could burn down. Struck by lightning maybe? Or he could trip and fall under the wheels of a horse-drawn wagon. Or maybe he could be cleaning his gun and it went off accidentally . . . There are all kinds of accidents, endless in fact.'

John pushed Ringwald through the door which led to a reception area and banged on a bell on the desk. Thomas Ladd came through his office door and met them.

'Ladd, these men are forcing me to make my will. I won't have it, do you hear?'

'No one can force you, Mr Ringwald,' said Ladd. 'But it's always wise to leave your affairs in order. No one knows when they're going to die. It could happen at any time without warning.'

Ringwald was pushed ahead of them into Ladd's office and forced on to a chair by Pickering. Ringwald had been inside Ladd's office many times before and it seemed strange that Ladd was not obeying his orders this time.

'Now, Mr Ringwald,' Ladd began, 'I want you to tell me everything you own.'

Ringwald cut in quickly before Ladd could continue.

'You know darn well what I own. You've got a thick folder in your cabinet giving details of all my businesses, buildings and land. You can make me sit here for days and nights but I won't sign a will.'

All four men looked long and hard at Ringwald. They knew they could not force him to do it.

'Are you denying that Miss Trefina Pickering is your daughter?' Ladd asked him.

'How should I know?' Ringwald retorted.

'You can't deny there is the possibility that she is though, can you?' Ladd persisted.

'A possibility don't make it fact!' Ringwald raised his voice.

'Would you rather everything you own went to the government?' Pickering asked him. 'It will you know, if you deny having any next of kin.'

Ringwald gave a mirthless laugh.

'You know, I might just do that. Then I'll be remembered for being a patriotic American.' Ringwald stood up and turned towards the door.

'Get me outa here! I'm not signing a thing.'

17

Up in the hills Trefina had prepared something to eat for Ben and herself. The coffee was hot as she took it from the small fire she had built at the entrance to the cave and poured the liquid into two mugs.

Ben had been quite cheerful to begin with but as the day drew on Trefina was beginning to get worried about him.

'You don't look so good, Ben,' she said. 'In fact, you look pretty bad.' She placed her hand on Ben's forehead. 'Why, you're burning up!' she exclaimed.

'I've felt a lot better, I'll admit,' he told her. 'I'll be OK. I just need to rest up a spell. I'll be fine by tomorrow.'

Trefina gave him a sideways glance. 'I do hope so, Ben. There's not much I can do for you up here. If you're no better by morning then I'm taking you into town for a doctor to look at you.'

Ben shook his head. 'No, Trefina! No matter what happens to me, you're to stay here! You're safe here. When your pa comes for you, then I'll go into town, but not until then.'

'We'll see,' she said. 'Maybe if you take a nap it'll make you feel better. You should have rested up at Ringwald's ranch, not ridden so soon after being shot.'

Ben gave her a weak smile. 'I had to know if you were safe, Trefina. I couldn't have stayed there not knowing what had happened to you.'

'And I can't stay here if you get any worse,' she told him emphatically.

★ ★ ★

Mike pulled Ringwald by his arm into the sheriff's office. Macey and his friends greeted them enthusiasticily.

'Did he sign it?' Macey asked.

Mike shook his head. 'Nope.'

He pushed Ringwald towards the cell and took off the man's handcuffs. Pickering unlocked the cell door while Mike held a gun on those inside. Ringwald entered reluctantly to join his men. He watched as Pickering put the key into the pocket of his jacket.

Pickering turned his nose up. 'It's beginning to smell in here,' he commented.

Mike reholstered his gun and they went back into the sheriff's office.

'You know, Mr Pickering,' Macey began, 'we can't stay here for too long if we're to get the herd to Wichita. We've still some branding to do. We should leave by next week at the latest.'

Pickering nodded. 'I'll need a couple of you to stay here and watch the place. If you leave before the circuit judge gets here, you'd better make a written statement about how you were forced to do what Ringwald told you. Will you do that for me?' he asked.

'Sure, Mr Pickering. You'll have to help me with the spelling and that. I've never needed to do much writing,' Macey explained a little self-consciously.

'Of course.' Pickering smiled. 'But I must confess I'm not too good with words myself.'

Pickering found a sheet of paper in the drawer and decided he would do the writing and Macey and the others would sign it.

Half an hour later, after frequent questioning from John Pickering, he had written down everything the men could remember that Ringwald had done which had been against the law, including the murder of one of his men in that very room when the man had tried to give himself up to Pickering and Mike. All the men signed that what had been written was a true account.

'Are you men here all who worked for Ringwald, or are there still some with the herd?' Mike asked Macey.

'There are six more on the Ringwald ranch besides us six,' said Macey.

Mike looked at John. 'Could they

spare two men to stay here, John?' he asked.

'Just about.' He turned to the men. 'I'll see that the two who remain here get paid just the same. There'll need to be two on and two off to watch this place. It's gonna be a long two weeks waiting for the judge, I reckon.'

Mike knew it would seem that way. A lot could happen in two weeks.

'While Ringwald's locked up, I reckon it would be safe enough for Trefina to go back home now,' Mike suggested.

John thought for a moment before nodding his agreement.

'You go back home and I'll stay here with Jake and take care of things,' said Mike.

'OK. Thanks, Mike. You'd better have the key.' He handed it over.

Mike could see that his friend was eager to get back to Trefina and he was soon riding out of town.

'Anyone got a pack of cards?' Mike asked the cowboys.

'There's one in this drawer,' said Macey, looking forward to a game.

'I'm gonna lay these cards face down on the desk,' Mike began as he took the pack from him, 'and you all take it in turns to pick one up. The first ones to pick up the ace of hearts and the ace of spades, stay here with Jake and me. The rest of you can go back to the herd. OK?' he asked.

Macey looked at the rest of them. They all nodded their agreement to the plan.

Mike placed six cards at a time on the desk. As the two aces did not turn up, the six were put to one side. After a few sixes drew a blank, the next six contained an ace of hearts.

'I stay here,' said Ned Tibbs.

Two further sixes did not contain the required card, but the next one did.

'I stay here, too,' said Don Phillips, showing the ace of spades.

The four cowboys without the two aces stood up.

'See you in about eight weeks' time,

boys!' said one of them as they walked towards the door.

The remaining two raised their hand in acknowledgement.

Mike was not sure whether the two left behind were glad or sorry about the outcome of the cards. He would have preferred it if Macey had been one of the men staying behind as a guard. But perhaps it was for the best. Macey was a leader and one would be needed on the trail.

'Who's taking night duty?' Ned Tibbs asked.

Mike grinned. 'Shall we cut for it?' he asked. 'If I cut high, Jake and me'll do night shift. If you cut high, Ned, then you two do it. OK?'

The two cowboys nodded. It seemed fair enough to them.

It was Mike who drew a jack of clubs and Ned drew a two of diamonds.

'Seems like Jake and me are the lucky ones. We'll come back at six tonight until six in the morning. So long, boys!'

Jake and Mike left the two cowboys in charge for about five hours.

It was not long before Ned and Don were disturbed from their card-game by Ringwald, shouting for attention.

'Hey, you in there! This slop-bucket needs emptying!'

'No can do, Mr Ringwald,' Ned replied. 'We haven't got the cell key.'

They were subjected to a stream of colourful language which made the two guards grin from ear to ear.

'We need some water!' Ringwald yelled.

'You'll have some at six o'clock when the guard is changed. Keep quiet in there!'

'You'll pay for this!' Ringwald yelled back at them.

'Shut up!' Don replied, and turned back to the game.

★   ★   ★

Trefina was growing more worried about Ben by the minute. They only

173

had one horse between them and she didn't think she would be able to get Ben up into the saddle even if they had a horse each. If only her father or Mike would come and help her. She wished she knew what was happening in town and if Ringwald had been put behind bars.

It would be dark within three hours, she judged. She sighed as she realized that there was nothing she could do for Ben on her own.

Ben had been lying down for an hour and she could tell he was shivering. A fever had set in.

'Trefina, I'm so cold,' he wailed.

There was nothing for her to do but to lay beside him and cover them both with the blanket. The heat from her body might help, she thought. She knew Ben was in no condition to take advantage of her.

Trefina pulled back the blanket and lay beside him. She covered them both and put her right arm around him, snuggling up closer. He did not seem to know she was there and she was glad of this.

She could tell it was growing darker from the patch of sky beyond the entrance to the cave. It reminded her of the hole in the wall of the jail showing just a faint night sky when Mike Clancey rescued her. Her heart skipped a beat as she thought of him and a smile came to her lips as she remembered she was lying beside another man.

Trefina fell asleep within half an hour and a while later she awoke to the sound of a voice calling her name.

18

John Pickering called in at the ranch house for a horse for Trefina before riding up to the cave. He was looking forward to seeing her again. His heart felt heavy, however, at the thought of breaking it to her that she was Ringwald's daughter and not his own. How would she react? he wondered. Would she be angry that he had kept it from her all these years? Would she understand that it had not been her mother's fault that she had borne a child from a man other than himself? There were so many questions he had been asking himself on his ride from the town that he seemed to be sending himself crazy.

Trefina's mare was still at the Ringwald ranch, he remembered, as Ringwald had put her in front of him in the saddle as he made his escape into town. He picked out one of the smaller horses for her to ride from the corral.

There would only be about two hours left of daylight, he realized as he looked up at the sky. It would mean he would have to stay the night in the cave and make the descent in the morning.

He reached the cave entrance and dismounted. He walked inside and all was quiet. Then he saw with horror that Trefina was asleep under the same blanket as Ben Haines.

Had she encouraged him? he wondered. Was this what had happened when Ringwald came to the house to see Julia all those years ago? Did he take her by force, or did she accept his advances willingly? If so, was her daughter acting the same way? What had Julia's real feelings been for Ringwald?

'Trefina!'

The girl stirred and turned towards the voice.

'Pa! I'm so glad to see you!'

'Are you sure of that?' he demanded gruffly.

'Oh, Pa!' she said, realizing that he had misinterpreted what he saw. 'Ben's real sick. He was shivering with a fever. I had to keep him warm somehow. You needn't worry, Ben's in no condition to . . . to touch me.'

John gave a sigh of relief and allowed a small smile to show on his lips.

Trefina got to her feet and pulled her father's arm so he could feel Ben's brow.

John nodded grimly. 'He sure is a sick young man. We'll have to wait until morning before we try and move him. I reckon I'll have to go to the house for the wagon. We can't bring it up here, but we can put him in it at the bottom of the hill once we've got him that far. It's gonna be difficult getting him on a horse. Once we do, I think you'd better sit behind him in the saddle and keep him from falling off.'

'Yes, Pa. I hope he's going to be OK.'

Pickering nodded. 'Trefina — I'm

178

sorry I thought the worst when I came here. I should have known better than to think you'd encourage Ben in any way.'

Trefina smiled and touched her father's arm. 'I understand, Pa. I forgive you. Are we taking Ben into town for a doctor? He sure needs one right now.'

'Yes. I'll leave you at the house and take him in. Ringwald's under lock and key, so he won't be bothering you. Let's get some sleep. You can keep Ben warm for the night.'

Trefina nodded and returned to the bunk beside Ben. John fetched a blanket from his horse and used it to cover himself on the floor of the cave.

The next morning Ben seemed a trifle better, but John and Trefina still thought he needed the attentions of a doctor. After a snatched breakfast they somehow got Ben into the saddle of his horse and John held him on until Trefina got up behind him. There was now a spare horse which John led whilst mounted on his own.

At the bottom of the hill John helped Trefina to get Ben from the saddle and on to the ground.

'I'll fetch the wagon,' said John.

'I'm coming into town with you, Pa. If Ringwald's locked up like you said, then I can see no reason not to help you with Ben.'

John mounted his horse and looked down at Trefina thoughtfully.

'OK. You can ride in the wagon with Ben and I'll drive it. I'll put some hay down to soften the jolts along the way.'

Trefina sat on the ground and held Ben's head in her lap. She realized that she hadn't looked at him fully before. Her mind had been too much on Mike Clancey to pay this man much attention. He was ordinary enough to look at. But the longer she studied him, the more she realized he had a kind, honest face. He was someone anyone could trust with their life.

An hour passed and just before her father returned, Ben opened his hazel eyes and looked up into Trefina's dark ones.

'Where am I?' he asked her. He still had his head in her lap. Had he died and gone to heaven?

'We're waiting for Pa to come with the wagon and we're taking you into town for a doctor,' she explained.

'There's no need for that,' he said. His voice was almost a whisper. Trefina could tell he was not feeling very strong.

'I don't want any arguments from you, Ben Haines!' she scolded. 'I'm not having you die on me after I kept you warm all night.'

Ben's mouth opened wide. 'You did that for me?' he asked. 'Wow! I didn't even know.'

'Thank goodness!' Trefina laughed.

Trefina could see her father and the horse-drawn wagon approaching.

'We'll soon have you attended to properly,' she said.

When John reached them and saw that Ben seemed slightly better, he realized that he would not be able to tell Trefina that she was not his daughter without being overheard. One thing he did not want was for her to find out the truth from someone else before he had the chance to tell her gently, privately. He knew it would be a shock and would take time for her to take it all in.

★   ★   ★

Back in Ringwald it was six o'clock in the morning. Mike and Jake had taken night watch over the men locked in the cell. They had been reasonably quiet during the night. There had been a few arguments as to whose turn it was to lie on the two bunks. The rest of them had to content themselves with the hard floor. The slop-pail was by now full to the brim. Mike realized that it would have to be emptied or the prisoners would come down with some disease.

'Hold your gun on 'em, Jake, while one of 'em brings out the pail to empty.'

Jake followed Mike into the jail.

'Ringwald, stand at the back of the cell. You there,' he pointed to one of the men, 'pick up that pail and bring it out. No tricks now, or it'll be your last. My finger feels a bit itchy on the trigger.'

Mike waited until Ringwald had obeyed his order, then unlocked the cell. The man chosen for the job picked up the heavy, smelly pail and came out of the cell with it. Mike locked the cell door behind him.

'Tell my lawyer that he can make up my will. I'll call round and sign it when it's ready,' Ringwald called out to the retreating three men.

'OK, Ringwald. I'll tell him. Smart decision,' Mike called back at him.

'Keep an eye on the office, Jake. Don and Ned should be here in a few minutes — or I'd like to know the reason why not.'

Mike followed the prisoner carrying the pail. The man was only too aware that a gun was pointing at his back.

'Round the corner to the cesspit,'

Mike told the man. 'And don't spill any! We don't want to infect the whole town now, do we?'

The prisoner did not reply. He half-made a plan to somehow get away, but thought better of it. He knew what the outcome would be if he did attempt an escape.

Mike followed the man back to the sheriff's office, by which time Don and Ned had arrived for their shift.

'Morning, boys!' Mike smiled at the two. 'Did you have a good night?'

'Yeah. Slept like a log,' Don replied.

'Me, too,' said Ned.

'Good. Don't let your guard down. They might try to trick you into letting them out. You won't be able to, of course. I've got the key.' He held it up and replaced it in his vest-pocket.

Mike ushered the prisoner back to the cell and Jake followed, gun at the ready, to make sure they did not rush them when the cell door was unlocked.

'We've bought breakfast for them in there,' said Ned as Mike and Jake returned to the sheriff's office.

Mike cast his eyes over the black cauldron containing hot gruel. There were also some dishes, spoons and a large pot of coffee on a tray. He nodded.

'Remember what I said, boys. Don't trust 'em an inch. Have a good day.'

Jake followed Mike outside.

'Breakfast I think, Jake?'

'Sure thing, Mike.'

Later on that morning Mike and Jake called in at the lawyer's office and told him to prepare Ringwald's will ready for him to sign. Mike still did not trust Thomas Ladd. His eyes looked shifty.

'I'll have it ready by two this afternoon,' Ladd told him. 'I'd like to see my client alone.'

Mike thought about it for a second or two, then said, 'You'll need a witness to the signature. I think that's what happens when someone makes a will. Am I right?'

'Yes. But I would still like to see my client alone before he signs.'

'What for?' Mike asked him. 'So you

can slip him a gun or something? I'll be straight with you, Mr Ladd. I don't trust you one little bit.'

Mike noticed the man's eyes avoiding his. A sure sign that he could not be trusted, Mike thought.

'Bring Mr Ringwald around about two then,' said the lawyer.

Mike nodded and he and Jake left the office.

'We'd better let Don and Ned know we're collecting Ringwald this afternoon.'

'Unless Ringwald's changed his mind again,' Jake smiled.

'Oh, I don't think so. He'll be glad enough to get out of that cell for a while. It's a mite cramped in there.'

When Ringwald heard that he was to see his lawyer at two, he found it hard to wait that long in the confines of the cell with no room to move around. At the same time, he had the feeling that he might not be returning there. He was sure he could rely on Ladd to come up with some plan.

19

It was 1.30 in the afternoon when John and Trefina Pickering entered the town of Ringwald with the injured Ben Haines.

'How are you feeling, Ben?' Trefina asked the young cowboy who lay on the straw in the wagon.

'Don't you worry about me, Miss Trefina. I promise you I ain't gonna die.'

'I should think not indeed!' Trefina answered with a smile. 'Just a few minutes longer and the doctor will see to you.'

Doctor Bryant's surgery and two-bed hospital was at the end of the street and the wagon and three occupants soon arrived outside.

'I'll go in first to see if the doctor's there. He might be out on a call.'

Trefina waited in the wagon with Ben

and a moment or two later John Pickering came out, followed by Bryant. The doctor helped John get Ben into his surgery.

'How long ago did this happen?' Bryant asked as he and John laid Ben on one of the two beds.

'A couple of days ago, Doc,' John answered. 'He was shot by Ringwald at his ranch. Ringwald had my . . . Trefina here held prisoner so I'd sell him my ranch. Ben received a slug when Ringwald rode off with her to the jail. A man named Mike Clancey and my employee Jake and young Ben here had gone to the ranch to get Trefina back. Mike Clancey helped her to escaped by the back way.'

Pickering did not give any more details. It could wait until the doctor had examined Ben.

'The wound's bled a little,' he said. 'It's been well bandaged. Who did it — you, young lady?' he asked Trefina.

Ben answered for her.

'It was Ringwald's housekeeper,

Tilda. She told me to rest up but I had to know how Miss Trefina was. I thought Ringwald might have killed her.'

Bryant nodded. 'She gave you wise advice, young feller. Pity you didn't listen to her.'

'He was real bad last night, Doctor. He was burning up, yet he was shivering with cold. I think maybe the fever's down a bit now though.'

Bryant undid the bandage, cleaned the wound and applied a new dressing. He mixed a powder into a glass of water and told Ben to drink it down.

'You can stay here until tomorrow, then we'll see how you are,' Bryant told him.

The smile Trefina gave him before she left made Ben feel better already. He could not wait until the next time he saw her.

Bryant saw John and Trefina to the door and left them in the street wondering what their next move was.

'We'd better find Mike and Jake,' said

John. 'I'll look in at the sheriff's office. You'd better stay outside until I know what's happening.'

As John entered the office, Trefina saw Mike and Jake coming towards her. Her face lit up with pleasure.

'I thought you'd be up at the cave, Trefina!' Mike said.

'We had to bring Ben Haines to the doctor. He was pretty bad last night. I'm sure he'll pull through OK though. What's going on, Mike?'

'We're taking Ringwald to the lawyer. He's gonna make out his will.'

Trefina frowned. 'Why? Who's he leaving everything to? I didn't know he'd got any kin.'

Mike and Jake exchanged glances. John had obviously not told Trefina that she was Ringwald's next of kin.

'Come on, you two. What's going on?' she repeated.

'It's a bit complicated, Miss Trefina,' said Jake uneasily.

'I told you to cut out the 'miss' from now on,' Trefina told him a little sternly.

As no one seemed as if they were going to tell her any more, she shrugged her shoulders.

'OK. You'll tell me when you're good and ready I guess. There's no chance that he'll grab me again, is there?'

Mike shook his head. 'We'll see to it that he won't ever touch you again.'

At that moment John came out of the sheriff's office. His face brightened at the sight of Mike and Jake, then he looked quickly from one to the other. Mike guessed what he was thinking and shook his head, reassuring John that he had not told Trefina who she really was.

'Pa, are we staying in town tonight?' Trefina asked.

'Yes, I think we deserve a bit of comfort for one night,' John replied.

'Oh good!' Trefina enthused. 'I could have a bath. I haven't washed for days.'

John smiled patronizingly at her. Tonight, when they were alone, he would have to tell her the truth about her real father — something that everyone seemed to know except Trefina herself.

'Are you taking Ringwald to the lawyer right now, Mike?' she asked.

'Yeah. Maybe you'd best not be here when we come out,' Mike suggested.

Trefina stood her ground.

'I want to see him in handcuffs. Better still, I'd like to see him hang.'

She turned to John and said, 'Ringwald should make you his beneficiary, Pa, after all the trouble he's caused us.'

Mike and John looked at each other again in the same way as before and Trefina knew they were hiding something from her.

Mike and Jake went into the sheriff's office and a moment or two later they came out with Ringwald, handcuffed, in front of them.

John pulled Trefina away a few feet so there was no chance of him touching her.

Ringwald stopped and looked hard at Trefina. The others wondered what his thoughts were as he studied her carefully. Did he now acknowledge her as his daughter? Before he had wanted her to give him a child. Could it possibly be true that he already had one — the young woman standing before him?

'Trefina . . . ' he began.

'Come on, Ringwald, you've got an appointment,' Mike broke in.

'Yeah.' The rancher almost sighed. 'To sign my death-warrant. Trefina, I'm sorry I hit you back there at my ranch. If I'd only known . . . '

Mike pushed him away and up the street before he could utter another word. He knew it must not come out here in the street, but somewhere quiet without watching eyes and listening ears.

Trefina found her heart was beating quickly. Something had happened between her and Ringwald in that one second. His eyes seemed to be pleading with her as if he wanted to tell her something.

John noticed the bewildered look on Trefina's face as she watched Ringwald being taken to the lawyer. He had expected to see hatred in her eyes for the man, but this was something very different.

'Come on, Trefina, let's book ourselves a couple of rooms at the hotel and relax a little. We've had enough upheavals to last for ages. But first, we'll put the horse in the stables for the night.'

★   ★   ★

Ringwald, followed close behind by Mike and Jake, entered Thomas Ladd's office.

'I'd like to see my client alone,' Ladd told them.

'Sorry, Mr Ladd, but I can't allow it. It's only a matter of signing the will and we'll be outa here.'

'But Mr Ringwald has the right to see me alone,' Ladd said indignantly.

'Mr Ringwald forfeited his rights a

long time ago. I aim to get him in front of the judge, and by golly, I'll do just that.'

'But what harm can it do?' Ladd pleaded.

'Maybe a lot of harm,' said Mike. 'You might even allow him to escape.'

Ladd drew in his breath. Mike could see the lawyer was getting more angry by the minute.

'I'm a man of the law. My word should be good enough to you that I'll not allow him to escape.'

Mike shook his head slowly.

'Ringwald's been a long-time client of yours, Mr Ladd. Although Mr Pickering has paid you a retainer, I'm sure your allegiance is still with Ringwald here. Now sit down and let him sign the damn will!'

Mike and Jake sat on either side of Ringwald and in front of Ladd. The parchment was pushed towards Ringwald, a pen freshly dipped into the inkwell, produced.

'I'll have to read it first,' said

Ringwald, indicating with the back of his hand that Ladd take the pen away for a moment.

They all waited while Ringwall read it to himself.

'What about your housekeeper — Tilda, isn't it?' Mike asked. 'Has she been paid lately? She deserves some compensation for working for you over the years. She'll be out of a job now.'

Ringwald looked at his lawyer for a moment. He knew he had to see the man again. Next time maybe Ladd would have thought of a way for him to escape?

'I'll think about it,' Ringwald said.

'You could sign it, Mr Ringwald, then come back again and insert a codicil.'

'What's that?' Mike asked.

Ladd gave him a withering look to belittle him.

'A codicil, sir, is something added after the will has been signed.'

Mike nodded his understanding and was irritated by Ladd's condescending manner.

'OK,' said Mike. 'I know this is only a reason to get outa jail again, but mebbe you do need the exercise, Ringwald. Now sign it and make it quick!'

'I can't,' said Ringwald. 'You'll need to take the cuffs off.'

Mike shook his head again. 'You can manage OK. Now sign!'

Ringwald looked at all three in turn, decided it was useless to argue, and signed everything he owned over to Trefina.

'I'll need your signature, too, Mr er . . .'

'Clancey will do,' said Mike.

'Just to witness that this is Mr Ringwald's signature. You can write your name, can't you?'

Ringwald grinned at this.

Mike thought for a moment. 'I reckon I can remember.'

20

John and Trefina booked two rooms next to each other and both ordered a bath in their rooms. They climbed the stairs and on the landing John waited outside his door.

'I've got something I want to tell you, Trefina,' he said quietly. 'Come into my room until the baths and water arrive.'

Trefina looked up at her father. She could tell from his expression that what he was about to say was of some importance. Trefina unlocked her door and left it open then followed John into his room.

'Sit down.' He ushered her to the one chair while he sat on the edge of the single bed.

Trefina sat. A frown came to her brow as she waited for her father's next words.

'I didn't ever want you to know this,

Trefina, but now it must be told. By now everyone in town will have heard what I am about to tell you and it's best it comes from me before someone else says anything to you.'

John hesitated for a few seconds before continuing.

'Trefina, I'm not your real father. I feel like I am and you'll always be a daughter to me, but . . . someone took your mother one night while I was in town. Do you understand what I'm saying?'

Trefina nodded. John could see the colour had drained from her face.

'Was Mother willing?' she asked, hoping that it was not true.

'No. She was upset for quite a while but wouldn't tell me why. Your mother and I couldn't seem to have any children and when I knew she was with child I was the happiest man alive. But I had a feeling, especially when you got older, that maybe you were not my daughter. Julia didn't tell me what had happened until the day she died.'

'And you didn't tell me until twenty years later.' Her voice was harsh, but trembling. She stood up.

'I'm going to my room now,' she told him. She seemed cold and distant and John wanted to hold her close and comfort her, but he didn't.

'Wait, Trefina! Don't go like this!' John pleaded. 'We'll have supper together after we've bathed.'

She did not turn to face him, but called over her shoulder, 'Suddenly, I don't feel at all hungry. I'll see you in the morning.'

Usually she would have added, 'Pa', and John knew she could not bring herself to call him that any more.

★ ★ ★

Mike and Jake turned up at the sheriff's office punctually at six o'clock that evening. They had brought the prisoners' supper with them. Ned and Don exchanged pleasantries with them, then left until six the next morning.

The prisoners were hungry and snatched at the plates of food doled out to them from the cauldron, and the mugs of coffee.

Ringwald was last to come to the bars and took the food and drink grudgingly.

'I've decided to leave something to my housekeeper,' he said. 'Ask Ladd to insert five hundred dollars into the will.'

Mike sniffed. 'Are you sure you can spare that much?' he asked him with sarcasm.

'Why, am I being too generous?' Ringwald smirked.

'Not generous enough. I guess that poor woman has worked for you for only a few cents a day.'

Ringwald gave a short laugh. 'Actually, not even that,' he said. 'She was glad of a roof over her head and food in her mouth.'

Mike turned to leave.

'You stingy old devil!' he growled, and shut the door behind him.

About half an hour later there was a

hullabaloo in the cells. A fight had broken out between two of the prisoners. Mike looked across at Jake who was sitting opposite him at the desk, holding a good hand of cards.

'Shut the noise in there!' Mike shouted, but the fight continued. Mike gave a long sigh and put his hand face down on the desk. Jake picked them up and quickly put them back.

Mike pulled his gun just in case this was a trick for him to open the cell door.

Ringwald was lying on one of the bunks, propped up by his elbows.

'Aren't you gonna do anything about it?' he asked with a sly grin on his face.

Mike shrugged his shoulders. 'Should I?' he asked. 'They're getting some exercise ain't they?'

He looked up at the square hole high up in the wall of the cell. No one had tried to escape from there, he noticed. Without help from outside, they wouldn't get very far, he reckoned. He doubted if any one of them could push through the hole, not like Trefina, who was small and slim.

'Good night, boys!' Mike called as he turned back to the door. 'Don't make too much noise in here, you'll disturb Mr Ringwald. I notice he don't take turns at sleeping on the floor. I should have a word with him about it if I were you.'

★ ★ ★

Mike and Jake were relieved at six the next morning and went for some breakfast before taking a nap in their room at the hotel. They slept until noon, then paid Thomas Ladd another visit to tell him to insert the bequest to Ringwald's housekeeper, Tilda, into Ringwald's Will.

At two, the pair called at the jail, carrying the prisoners' food. They were then to take Ringwald to the lawyer.

As they were walking towards Ladd's office with Ringwald, handcuffed, walking in front of them, they noticed

Trefina and John Pickering coming from the hotel. Mike gave them a cheery wave, but he noticed, even from a distance, that Trefina was not looking too happy. He guessed that John had told her the truth about herself the night before.

It was at that moment that a horse and buggy came rushing towards them with a frantic woman in the driver's seat. Mike could tell the animal had spooked and was out of control. Mike considered trying to grab the horse's reins, as it passed, but at the speed it was going, he knew he would only be pulled off his feet.

The animal and the terrified woman sped past them. Mike thought fast.

'Keep your eye on this one, Jake,' he said.

Mike ran to a horse tied up outside the general store, leapt aboard the saddle and gave chase to the retreating buggy.

Just then a man came out of the store carrying some parcels. He dropped them on the boardwalk and ran into the road, his gun drawn from its holster.

'Come back here with my horse!' he called.

'Don't shoot at him, mister!' Jake pleaded. 'He's after a bolting horse and buggy with a lady on board.'

Jake had instinctively moved towards the man and Ringwald took this opportunity to act. He shoved Jake into the man with great force and both fell to the ground in a cloud of dust.

Ringwald grabbed Jake's gun and ran in the direction of the rear of the buildings down an alley. He turned and fired the weapon, but the bullet whined between the two men who were getting up from the ground.

'Let me borrow your gun, mister,' Jake pleaded. 'He mustn't get away.'

'That's Mr Ringwald, ain't it?' the man asked.

'That's right, mister. He's awaiting trial. Your gun!'

The man reluctantly handed the weapon over to Jake.

Jake followed in the direction Ringwald had taken. He wished Mike was there. He knew he was too old to go chasing after a fugitive, and he was no gunman either.

Mike returned to the spot where he had left Jake and Ringwald. The horse had calmed down by now, but the woman still looked shaky and flustered.

'That's my horse,' the man told Mike.

Mike dismounted and handed him the reins.

'Thanks for the loan.' He grinned. 'Where's my prisoner and Jake?'

The man pointed in the direction both men had gone.

'Thank you, young man!' the woman called after his retreating back. Mike raised his arm in acknowledgement and hurried on.

'Mike! Over here!'

Mike looked towards the voice and saw Jake's head pop out from behind a water-barrel.

'He's gone into the livery,' Jake informed him.

'I hope he don't ride off with Thunder,' said Mike.

They crept forward, keeping their eyes on the stable door and also at an opening up in the hay-loft. Mike guessed Ringwald would have climbed the ladder he had used to help rescue Trefina. He was proved right when a bullet came from the hay loft. They dodged out of the firing-line.

'Is there another way out apart from this one?' Mike asked Jake.

'I don't think so.' Jake shook his head. 'I've never investigated the place before though,' he admitted.

John and Trefina had witnessed what had happened and John touched Trefina's arm.

'Stay here, Trefina!' he told her. 'I must help Mike and Jake.'

'Pa, no!' Trefina almost shouted.

John looked at her and a smile came to his face. She still thought of him as her father. He felt glad.

'I know you've got to go, Pa. But before you do, who is my real father? Do you know?'

Pickering nodded slowly and his face looked sad.

'It's Ringwald,' he admitted.

He looked at her shocked face one more time, then ran off towards his two good friends.

Trefina sat on a bench outside the general store and waited.

21

Mike and Jake turned when they heard approaching feet. They saw it was John Pickering.

'John, he's in the hay-loft. Keep out of the line of fire!' Mike urged.

John came up beside the two men.

'I saw what happened, Mike,' John told him. 'If Jake here hadn't been so intent on stopping the feller whose horse you borrowed from shooting you, he would have kept a better eye on Ringwald.'

Jake took this as a reprimand.

'I'm sorry, Mr Pickering. I guess I'm gettin' too old for this kind of thing nowadays.'

Mike put his hand on the old man's shoulder.

'Losing Ringwald — temporarily — is better than getting a bullet in my back,' Mike told him.

Pickering looked from one to the other.

'What happens now, Mike?'

'You two keep an eye on the loft up there.' Mike pointed. 'I'll go inside the stable and somehow get him down.'

'Be careful, Mike,' Pickering warned.

Mike grinned. 'Don't you worry none. I intend to be.'

John and Jake watched with bated breath as Mike ran with head down low, across to the stable from their hiding-place opposite. They saw him inch his way to the door, all the time looking up at the loft. Mike half-expected a bullet from above, but guessed that Ringwald was saving his ammunition until he could get a sure target.

As Mike entered the stable, Thunder gave him a welcoming nicker. He looked up above him to the loft.

'Come on down, Ringwald! You can't stop up there for ever.'

There was no reply and no sound.

'You won't get fed up there. I'm quite

willing to wait for you,' Mike shouted up.

Again there was no sound. Mike did not like it. He realized that Ringwald was still handcuffed and would not have as much dexterity with his hands. All the same, he would still be able to fire a gun, handcuffed or not.

Mike sat down with his back to one of the stalls. His position was obscured by one of the roof-supports. He would be able to keep an eye on the loft, but at the same time he would be relatively safe from one of Ringwald's bullets.

As he waited, Mike took the opportunity to fill any empty chamber in his gun with bullets. He wondered how many Ringwald had in his.

Half an hour passed and there was still no sight nor sound of Ringwald. Mike was beginning to get slightly worried. But then that was probably Ringwald's intention. He hoped John and Jake would not put themselves in any danger where they were.

Trefina had grown tired of waiting.

She knew she should stay where she was, but she had to know if everything was all right. She walked down the alley leading to the stables and spied her father and Jake behind a pillar.

She thought about calling them but realized their attention would be drawn away from the loft where their eyes were fixed. She came up to them quietly and they both jumped in surprise.

'Trefina!' John said angrily. 'I told you to keep out of the way!'

'Sorry, Pa,' she said. 'I couldn't wait any longer. The suspense was killing me. Is Ringwald up there?' she asked. 'Where's Mike?'

'We think Ringwald's still in the loft. Mike went inside a while back and we haven't heard from him since.'

Trefina nodded. After a few seconds she added, 'Don't you think one of you should go in and find out what's happening?'

John and Jake exchanged looks.

'Mebbe she's right, Mr John,' said

Jake. 'I'll go if you want?'

John shook his head. 'No, you stay here with Trefina. I'll go.'

They watched as he hurried across to the stables and went inside.

As this happened, a few of the townsfolk came up to them.

'Is Ringwald holed up in the stables?' the man whose horse Mike had borrowed to save the woman in the buggy asked.

'Yeah,' Jake answered. 'All's quiet at the moment. I don't know how long it'll be before there's gunfire in there. I should go back if I were you, folks. You might catch a stray bullet.'

As Jake said this he caught sight of Ben Haines coming towards them. Trefina saw him also and Haines received a big smile from her.

'Ben, get outa here!' Jake ordered. 'And take Trefina with you. All of you — go! You'll know what happens in a while.'

There were a few mumblings but the townsfolk realized they were only in the way where they were, and left the scene. Trefina caught hold of Ben's free arm and walked back to the street with him.

Mike waited quietly where he sat. Then he heard a rustling nearby. He thought it was probably one of the horses as he was sure that Ringwald was still in the loft. But he was wrong.

'Don't move, Lightning!' came Ringwald's voice. 'Don't turn around. Throw down your gun — now!'

Mike was angry with himself for being duped by the man. He knew that if he did throw down his gun, Ringwald would have no hesitation in shooting him.

'OK,' said Mike quietly. 'I'm taking it out of its holster now.'

He was pretty sure of the direction where Ringwald was hiding. He took the gun slowly from its holster and the next second he lay on his left side and brought his gun up and fired into the dimness of the stable. There was a sound from that direction as if Ringwald had been hit but did not want

Mike to know it.

There was a slight rustling sound to Mike's left and it moved around behind a stall. Mike waited, still lying on his stomach.

A few moments later Thunder came charging out of the stable with Ringwald on his back, clutching his mane. The horse was soon out of the door and in the open and was making for the street at speed.

Mike saw that Jake was about to fire on him but he shook his head and indicated with his left hand to put his gun away. Mike saw the old man frown.

Thunder heard a shrill whistle which he had come to know was his master calling him. All four hoofs stopped suddenly but the momentum caused Ringwald to fly over the animal's head. There came the sound of crunching bones and Mike winced.

Jake and Mike ran up to the now stationary horse and inspected the former rider. Ringwald was still alive, but only just, Mike reckoned.

'Trefina.' Ringwald's voice was so quiet it was barely audible. 'My daughter,' he whispered.

'Jake, go and fetch Trefina! Quick!'

The old man reholstered the gun and ran as fast as he was able towards the street. Ben and Trefina were sitting on the bench outside the general store.

'Trefina! Come quick! Ringwald wants to speak to you before he dies.'

Trefina got up and hurried towards the stables, followed by Jake and Ben.

She saw him lying where he had fallen. He looked grubby and unkempt, and much older than he had a few days earlier. His days spent in the jail had taken its toll on him, and for a few seconds, Trefina actually felt sorry for the man whom she now knew to be her father.

She bent down beside him. His hand moved slightly and Trefina knew he wanted her to take it, which she did.

'Sorry,' he whispered. 'Forgive . . . me.'

Before Trefina could answer him, his

head fell to one side and she knew he was dead.

John helped her to her feet and held her close to him. He could feel her trembling.

'It's all over, Pa,' she said quietly.

He held her away from him and looked down at her face. A tear was not far away. Was she shedding tears for the man who was her real father in sorrow, or relief?

'Pa,' she began, 'he may have been my father, but *you* have always been my real father to me, and always will be. I love you, Pa.'

Mike looked at Ben Haines and knew that Haines wished Trefina was in his arms at that moment. He had a feeling it would not be too long before his wishes came true.

Some of the townsfolk came running up and saw Ringwald lying in the dust. A spokesman came up to Mike.

'Mr . . . Clancey, is it?' he asked.

'I go by that name,' Mike replied.

'Some of us have been talking. We

want you to be our sheriff.'

A slow smile came to Mike's lips.

'I won't be around for much longer,' he said. 'The next sheriff you get should be elected, not installed. Get someone to fetch the undertaker.'

★　★　★

The circuit judge arrived in town and the prisoners were given a trial. Each received five years in the Texas Penitentiary.

John Pickering's house was partly rebuilt with Mike, Ben and Jake's help, and was now habitable again.

'Oh well,' said Mike. 'It's time to say goodbye.'

'No!' Trefina ran to him and held his arms. 'You can't leave us. We need you.'

Mike shook his fair head and smiled.

'No, you don't. Not any more. You're a rich woman now, Trefina. And with it, you'll have power. Use it wisely.'

'I will, Mike. Thank you for everything. I hope you find what you're looking for. We all wish you all the best.'

Mike mounted the big black gelding and looked down at his four friends. Tilda, Ringwald's housekeeper came out of the house and stood beside Jake. Mike grinned. They made a nice couple.

With a final wave, he was riding out of their lives.

THE END

We do hope that you have enjoyed reading this large print book.

Did you know that all of our titles are available for purchase?

We publish a wide range of high quality large print books including:
**Romances, Mysteries, Classics
General Fiction
Non Fiction and Westerns**

Special interest titles available in large print are:
**The Little Oxford Dictionary
Music Book, Song Book
Hymn Book, Service Book**

Also available from us courtesy of Oxford University Press:
**Young Readers' Dictionary
(large print edition)
Young Readers' Thesaurus
(large print edition)**

For further information or a free brochure, please contact us at:
**Ulverscroft Large Print Books Ltd.,
The Green, Bradgate Road, Anstey,
Leicester, LE7 7FU, England.
Tel:** (00 44) **0116 236 4325**
Fax: (00 44) **0116 234 0205**

HARD RIDE TO LARGO

Jack Holt

When Jack Danner arrived in Haley Ridge he spent the night in jail. But then financier Spencer Bonnington offers him fifteen hundred dollars to escort Sarah, his niece, to her father's ranch in Largo. However, their journey is fraught with danger, especially when Bob Rand and his partners see Sarah as a prize and a means of ransom from the Bonningtons. Danner is being watched, but by whom? An easy fifteen hundred becomes the hardest money he's ever earned.

MOON RAIDERS

Skeeter Dodds

Wayne Creek is a family town, not overly prosperous. However, when Samuel Lane arrives with his own enrichment in mind, change is anticipated. Though the town might find affluence through him, it would also become dangerous, with the dregs of the West flooding in . . . Standing alone against Lane is Jeb Tierney. The scales of justice seem to be loaded against him — and yet nothing is quite as it seems. Will Lane, after all, get his much-deserved comeuppance?

THE SHERIFF OF RED ROCK

H. H. Cody

Jake Helsby figured there would be trouble as the rider headed into town. It had started when somebody put a piece of lead into Fred at his place, the Circle B. One of the hands reckoned the Grissom kid was responsible, but Jake was suspicious of the mayor's anxiety to hang the suspect, and of Lily Jeffords's interest in the kid's well-being. And even as he searched for the true culprit, Jake had his own dark secret to protect . . .

BAD MOON OVER DEVIL'S RIDGE

I. J. Parnham

Sheriff Cassidy Yates rides into Eagle Heights only to land in jail on an unfounded murder charge. Although Cassidy answers the charge, his wayward brother becomes implicated in the murder and the kidnapping of the dead man's widow. In a town gripped by a conspiracy of fear, Cassidy is helped by a newspaper correspondent to find the real killer and the kidnapped woman. But gun-toting ranchers and hired guns stand between Cassidy and justice — can he prove his brother's innocence?